Darlene Bargmann

It's All About Emily

A Novel

JustFiction Edition

Impressum/Imprint (nur für Deutschland/only for Germany)
Bibliografische Information der Deutschen Nationalbibliothek: Die Deutsche Nationalbibliothek verzeichnet diese Publikation in der Deutschen Nationalbibliografie; detaillierte bibliografische Daten sind im Internet über http://dnb.d-nb.de abrufbar.

Alle in diesem Buch genannten Marken und Produktnamen unterliegen warenzeichen-, marken- oder patentrechtlichem Schutz bzw. sind Warenzeichen oder eingetragene Warenzeichen der jeweiligen Inhaber. Die Wiedergabe von Marken, Produktnamen, Gebrauchsnamen, Handelsnamen, Warenbezeichnungen u.s.w. in diesem Werk berechtigt auch ohne besondere Kennzeichnung nicht zu der Annahme, dass solche Namen im Sinne der Warenzeichen- und Markenschutzgesetzgebung als frei zu betrachten wären und daher von jedermann benutzt werden dürften.

Coverbild: www.ingimage.com

Verlag: JustFiction! Edition ist ein Imprint der
LAP LAMBERT Academic Publishing GmbH & Co. KG
Heinrich-Böcking-Str. 6-8, 66121 Saarbrücken, Deutschland
Telefon +49 681 37 20 310, Telefax +49 681 37 20 310-9
Email: info@justfiction-edition.com

Herstellung in Deutschland (siehe letzte Seite)
ISBN: 978-3-8454-4758-2

Imprint (only for USA, GB)
Bibliographic information published by the Deutsche Nationalbibliothek: The Deutsche Nationalbibliothek lists this publication in the Deutsche Nationalbibliografie; detailed bibliographic data are available in the Internet at http://dnb.d-nb.de.

Any brand names and product names mentioned in this book are subject to trademark, brand or patent protection and are trademarks or registered trademarks of their respective holders. The use of brand names, product names, common names, trade names, product descriptions etc. even without a particular marking in this works is in no way to be construed to mean that such names may be regarded as unrestricted in respect of trademark and brand protection legislation and could thus be used by anyone.

Cover image: www.ingimage.com

Publisher: JustFiction! Edition
is an imprint of the publishing house
LAP LAMBERT Academic Publishing GmbH & Co. KG
Heinrich-Böcking-Str. 6-8, 66121 Saarbrücken, Germany
Phone +49 681 37 20 310, Fax +49 681 37 20 310-9
Email: info@justfiction-edition.com

Printed in the U.S.A.
Printed in the U.K. by (see last page)
ISBN: 978-3-8454-4758-2

Copyright © 2012 by the author and LAP LAMBERT Academic Publishing GmbH & Co. KG and licensors
All rights reserved. Saarbrücken 2012

Table of Contents

Chapter 1- Emily Hanson, Sixth Grader…Pg. 3

Chapter 2- The Mean Girl…Pg. 10

Chapter 3- An Invitation…Pg. 16

Chapter 4- More Trouble…Pg. 23

Chapter 5- Lunch…Pg. 30

Chapter 6- After School…Pg. 34

Chapter 7- An Unexpected Friend…Pg. 38

Chapter 8- My Drama…Pg. 43

Chapter 9- The Truce…Pg. 47

Chapter 10- Sister Talk…Pg. 51

Chapter 11- Harvey Mall…Pg. 55

Chapter 12- Beth's Mom…Pg. 60

Chapter 13- Boys!…Pg. 64

Chapter 14- Bree's News…Pg. 71

Chapter 15- Deal Breaker…Pg. 75

Chapter 16- Carson…Pg. 78

Chapter 17- The Deal…Pg. 81

Chapter 18- Lizzie…Pg. 83

Chapter 19- Heartbreak…Pg. 86

Chapter 20- The Party…Pg. 88

For Sandra Prickett, Ashley Butrimavicius, and Ali McNabb

Chapter 1
Emily Hanson, Sixth Grader

On my first day of middle school, I woke up 12 minutes before my alarm was set to go off. I stared at the ceiling above my bed and wondered if middle school would be everything I dreamed. New friends, new teachers, new boys. New is always exciting. New is change and change means new experiences-good and bad. The question in my mind was, "Is this new experience going to be more good than bad?" Grade school was fun. My grades were fine, and that made my mom and dad happy, but what I really loved was hanging out with my friends and flirting with cute boys. There were a lot of cute boys in my grade school- no one cuter than Carson Wilde, who'd been my boyfriend in 5th grade. During the summer, though, we didn't talk at all. His family went on a cruise or something. Otherwise, we would have seen each other at church.

Before getting out of bed, I did what I always do when I'm nervous.

Good morning, God. Please watch over me today and don't let me do anything embarrassing.

My friend's mom, who is kind of new-agey, says to take a deep breath, exhale slowly through my mouth, and picture myself surrounded by a white light of positive energy. So, next I did that.

When my alarm went off, I felt ready to face the day whatever was in store. I nearly sprained my ankle getting out of bed. The first day of school was always exciting for me, but this one was special. I couldn't help wondering if people would like me. I was pretty sure I would have to prove myself to my teachers. I was, after all, the little sister of Eve Hanson, queen of screw ups.

As I was taking a shower, I realized that, in at least one class, I would have to get up and tell everyone what I did over the summer. My problem was, it had been a dull summer. We usually spend a couple weeks in Wisconsin Dells, but this year Eve said she would only go if her boyfriend, Price, could come with us. She put up such a fuss that my parents cancelled the whole trip. They told Eve that she would have to live with the guilt of disappointing her sisters. It didn't work. Eve didn't care. All she wanted was to be with Price, no matter who suffered the consequences. She'd been that way ever since she started going out with him. Price and his family live on the other side of town and my mom and dad are kind of stuck up about that. I think that's why Eve wanted to go out with him in the first place, to make our parents mad. Eve is just a mean-

Good morning again, God. Please forgive me for thinking bad things about Eve. I really do love her.

I figured I could always talk about going to the Dells last summer. We always stay at the same resort. Everyone in our family was a good swimmer, but my mom usually stays with Dana, my little sister, in the kiddie pool. Dana is nine and old enough to hang out in the regular pool, but she's deaf. Mom and Dad were too scared to leave her alone with a bunch of people who had no idea of her limitations. I get that, but I feel bad that Mom didn't get to dive, which is her favorite thing to do and she looks so graceful when she does it. My mom is definitely the most beautiful woman I've ever seen and that includes models and movie stars. Actually, the only woman who comes even close is my best friend's mom.

I studied myself in the full length mirror that used to belong to my grandma, but she didn't want it anymore because she can't stand looking at herself anymore. It's so silly because she is very pretty for her age. She is my mom's mom, after all.

I was pleased with my reflection. My hair looked especially awesome, make-up looked decent, and my new clothes fit perfectly. I smiled at myself and patted my shoulder for encouragement.

Good morning, God, breathe, white light of positive energy.

"I made pancakes, Em," my mom said, as I walked in the kitchen.

Dana was shoveling her pancakes in her mouth. I walked into her line of sight and said "Good morning, Dana" in sign language.

Dana smiled and made a letter "m" with her fingers and put her hand over her heart. That's how she says my name.

"You want one or two pancakes?" my mom asked me.

"I can't eat! I'm too nervous!" I whined.

"You are such a dork, Emily. It's just school," Eve said, walking into the room. She looked so good and had probably spent half as much time on her appearance as I had on mine.

"You have to eat something. How about some toast?" my mom said, ignoring her oldest daughter. My mom and dad found out long ago, that's the best way to handle Eve.

"I'm so nervous. I don't want to throw up. Please, Mom, don't make me eat!" I whined some more.

"I can't believe you're my sister," Eve said. She was painting her nails bright red. She knew Mom and Dad didn't like that. I think that's the reason she did it. It couldn't be because it looked good. Eve and I take after our mom, blond, almost white hair plus we live in Wisconsin. Those two things equal pale skin. Next to it, bright red nails look pretty gross. I always wear pastels. I had painted my nails lavender the night before to match the baby doll dress I was wearing.

Showing very little reaction to Eve's defiance, my mom calmly put a bottle of fingernail polish remover and a cotton ball on the table next to her. Since this is something that happens a lot, she had some handy. To me, she said, "Fine. I'm sure when you're tummy starts growling, the other kids will understand. You'll make lots of friends."

So, Mom wins again. I grabbed a plate and took two pancakes.

"I don't see why I can't wear what I want on my fingernails. They're MY fingernails!" Eve mumbled.

"We're not having this conversation again, Eve. Take it off," Mom said, calmly.

"Fine!" Eve exclaimed, rolling her eyes.

"You can use some of mine, Eve," I offered.

"Are you serious? What is that called? God-awful Grape?" Eve sneered.

"Watch yourself, Eve," my mom said, carrying a plate in one hand and pointing at Eve with the other. "This little attitude of yours has to go or no more Price. You understand?"

"Leave Price alone! I don't know why you and Daddy hate him so much. It's so unfair!" Eve exclaimed. "The apple doesn't fall far from the tree. Eat your breakfast and get going. You'll miss your bus." She was referring to Price's dad, who is a real jerk.

Eve made gagging noises when my mom put a plate of pancakes in front of her.

"I want a bagel. I'll just pick one up on the way to school. Sara's driving," Eve said, "Oh, I'll need some money for that bagel."

I grabbed my book bag, waved goodbye to Dana and headed out the door. It was the same every morning with Eve.

I practically ran to the bus stop. I probably would have if it hadn't been for my fear of vomiting in front of potential friends. I couldn't wait to see what my two best friends were wearing. They were already at the bus stop.

"Hey guys! Why do you both look so sad?" I exclaimed.

Bethany and Brianna have been my friends practically since birth. We grew up together in the same neighborhood and our parents are all friends. Beth's mom and my dad used to date in high school. I don't know why they broke up, but I know my mom and dad didn't meet until college. My mom isn't even from Harvey. She grew up in La Crosse. She and my dad went to college at the University of Wisconsin in Madison. Mary, Beth's mom, never went to college. She met her husband, Joe, at an art show in Willett, which is a city about an hour away from us. There is a lot of crime there. It's pretty much a party town. Anyway, Beth's mom went to this art show and she was admiring a contemporary sculpture when a man approached her and asked her what she thought. I don't know what she said, but he must have liked it. It was Beth's dad and he was the sculptor. I've heard the story a million times, but I wouldn't mind hearing it a million times more. It's so romantic.

Beth is a nice girl. She is happy when she's at home or with Brianna and me. At school, she is very shy and kind of sad. She's overweight and some kids are mean to her. Not all of them but enough to make her avoid parties or other situations that might upset her. I think if people don't like her because of her weight, it's their loss. She's so much fun and I couldn't ask for a better friend. In fifth grade, when Carson dumped me, she made me brownies and let me stay at her house and cry. She told me how much of a jerk Carson is and how dumb he was for dumping me, as if he could do any better. If it weren't for Beth, I probably would have been depressed for weeks.

Brianna, Bree for short, is also shy. She was one of only 6 black kids in our grade school and the only one in our grade. There were a couple of kids who teased her, called her names that they obviously heard from their red-neck parents, but mostly, nobody even pays attention to the color of her skin. I talked to my mom about it once and she said, "Some people think they know everything, but, really, they have a lot to learn." One of those people is Price's dad. I heard my mom call him a "bald headed bigot" once, then she laughed and said, "That was mean. I shouldn't have said that." She was just saying what everyone was thinking.

"Why do you look so happy?" Beth answered my question with a question.

"It's the first day of a new school! Don't you know what that means? New friends and new boys!" I exclaimed.

"New people to make fun of me," Beth said.

"We're back to being the babies of the school. Remember how happy we were to be fifth graders and the oldest kids in school? Well, we aren't anymore!" Brianna said.

Good morning, God. Breathe. Light of positive energy.

"Everyone's going to make fun of me," Beth said.

"No one is going to make fun of you. If you believe people will, then they will," I replied.

"You sound like my mom."

"That's where I got it, dodo. Oh, look, here comes the bus!" I said, excitedly.

Beth and Bree groaned.

"Oh, hey Beth. Your hair looks really good," I said.

She smiled and thanked me. I had said it to give her a little confidence, but I didn't lie. Beth's mom is a hairdresser and she always does Beth's hair. She always does a really good job. Beth's new haircut was short and stylish. Bree is always complaining about her hair. I wish Beth would ask her mom to give Bree some pointers.

An empty bus pulled up beside us and we climbed in.

Beth and Bree sat together and I sat alone. I was glad. I wanted someone new to sit next to me. I love meeting new people.

Unfortunately, I already knew everyone who climbed on the bus. Some of them said hello, and some of them looked like Beth and Bree, dreading school.

I waited anxiously for the bus to reach Dwayne Gordon's neighborhood. Dwayne is the son of a retired baseball player named Lefty Gordon, who used to play for the Milwaukee Brewers. Dwayne used to go to private school, but Beth's mom found out he was transferring to Harvey Middle School. Beth, Bree, and I never had the chance to meet him. I couldn't wait to introduce myself. Unfortunately, he didn't even look at me when he got on the bus.

"Oh my gosh! Did you see him? He is so cute!" Beth exclaimed, forgetting how nervous she was about starting school.

Brianna glanced back at him and shrugged. Beth and I knew she had a serious crush on him, but she would never admit it. She never talks about boys unless it is someone on television or in a movie.

The bus pulled up to the school and the parking lot was packed with kids from all over Harvey. So many cute boys!

Watch out Harvey Middle School. Here comes Emily Hanson, sixth grader.

Chapter 2
The Mean Girl

The zoo of people in the parking lot made me feel a little anxious, but it was a good kind of anxious, like I knew this year would be exciting and adventurous.

I guess I was lost in my own excitement, because as we were walking across the parking lot, I was looking in my compact mirror and I bumped into someone.

"How do I look? Is my hair ok?" I asked anyone who would listen when I ran into a girl, "Oh! Oh my gosh! I'm sorry!" I looked at the girl I'd run into. She was a pretty, black girl with long wavy hair. She was wearing a short, pink sweater and black hip huggers with a pink belt. She had a pink, beaded purse slung over her shoulder and I noticed she had matching nail polish. She looked awesome, and I would have told her so if she didn't look like she was about to hit me.

"Excuse you!" She exclaimed.

"I said I was sorry." The last thing I wanted was to make an enemy on the first day of school.

"Why don't you watch where you're going? News flash- you aren't the only one here," the girl said.

"I know that. I was just looking in the mirror. I didn't mean to bump into you."

"Maybe next time instead of staring at yourself, you'll watch where you're going," she said, and walked away.

"Wow. What just happened?" I asked.

"I think you just made a friend," Beth answered, sarcastically.

Good morning, God. Please watch over me and don't let me do anything else embarrassing. Breathe. Positive white light.

"Hey, Emily!" A scrawny, red haired girl carrying about a hundred notebooks and folders ran toward me. I didn't recognize her at first, but then I remembered meeting her once at my sister's boyfriend's birthday party. She had followed me around the entire time talking about some boy she liked. Most of the kids at the party were older than me, so I hung out with Lauren. I didn't really think I'd have to hang with her at school, though. She could ruin my chances at popularity.

Dear God, wow, I am so sorry I thought that. What a horrible thing to think!

"Hi Lauren," I said, not really interested in striking up a friendship, but feeling guilty for what I'd just thought.

"Isn't it great that we're going to the same school now?" Lauren asked, excitedly.

"Yeah. It's great. These are my friends Beth and Brianna."

"Hi! My name is Lauren McCloskey. My brother, Price, is going out with Emily's sister, Eve."

"Hi," Beth and Bree answered at the same time. They knew the name. Everyone knew the name McCloskey. Fame isn't always a good thing, though. Lauren's dad was well known for being an idiot, my dad says.

I looked around. There were so many guys! I already had counted 6 really cute ones and I suddenly felt like I looked funny so I pulled out my mirror again, this time careful not to bump into anyone.

The five minute bell rang and we checked our schedules. Brianna and I had Science together. We walked the halls of the school looking for our class, and tried not to look lost.

"Do you think we'll ever get the hang of this? I can't believe how big this school is," Bree said anxiously.

"It isn't that big. I'll bet within a week, we'll be walking around here like we own the place," I replied.

Finally we found room 3-32, where we would spend the year talking about amoebas, protons and where, I heard, we would dissect worms. Our teacher was Mr. Greesy. Over the summer, after registration day when we got our schedules, Eve told me she'd had Mr. Greesy for 8th grade Science. She said he liked to embarrass kids who don't pay attention. I made a mental note to pay attention to every word. There's nothing I hate more than embarrassment.

Mr. Greesy was standing outside his classroom, ushering kids in. He seemed irritated that he had to be there. That was something else Eve had said about him. He always looks irritated. I wondered why he chose to be a teacher.

"Check the seating chart. You have assigned seats. No exceptions!" he instructed.

Our class had kind of a funny smell and instead of desks, there were tables with weird silver levers sticking out on top. The chairs were tall, metal barstools.

"Wow! This looks so 'High School'! I love it!" I exclaimed.

Bree checked the seating chart and groaned. "I guess this means we can't sit together. I'm sitting next to someone named Jasmine Thomas. You're sitting next to some guy named Colin right over there," She said, pointing to a table.

I looked where she was pointing and saw Colin. He was cuter than any boy I'd gone to grade school with. He had dark hair and really tan arms, which probably meant he had gone somewhere on vacation, because people usually don't get very tan in Wisconsin, at least not by the actual sun.

"Oh my gosh, Bree! He is so cute!" I whispered, excitedly.

"Oh no. I can't believe this. Look who I'm stuck sitting next to," Bree said, but I wasn't really paying attention to her.

I walked quickly to my seat and didn't even notice when Brianna took her seat next to the same girl I'd bumped into in the parking lot.

"Hi, are you Colin?" I asked my table partner. He had chocolate brown eyes and the same color hair. He made my tummy feel funny.

He smiled. "Yeah, that's me. You're Emily?" I loved his smile. It was a little crooked.

Maybe it was my imagination or just wishful thinking, but he looked happy when he found out it was me he was seated next to.

I didn't hear anything Mr. Greesy said for about the first fifteen minutes of class. All I could think about was getting to know Colin and I wondered if he would like me. I didn't hear anything until Colin nudged my arm and asked, "Do you know her?" He motioned to Jasmine. She was laughing and pointing at me, talking to some people who sat around her.

"You got hairspray in your ears, princess?" she yelled. Everyone in class laughed except me, Colin, and Bree. I could feel my face turn red and I looked back at the teacher, who was also looking at me. The level of irritation in his face had doubled.

"Miss Hanson, I asked you to stand and tell the class a little bit about yourself," Mr. Greesy said.

"Oh, I'm sorry." I stood up and faced the class. "My name is Emily Hanson. I used to go to Cordelia A. P. Harvey Elementary School. I have two sisters. My older sister goes to Harvey High School and my little sister goes to Preston Special School, because she's deaf. My mom and dad are accountants. Umm…what else should I say?" I asked, embarrassed, trying not to look at Jasmine. I knew she was making fun of me.

"Tell us more about your little sister. How does she communicate with her family and teachers?" Mr. Greesy was way too interested in me, I thought.

"Well, we learned sign language and she's starting to read lips. She's getting pretty good at it, actually," I answered.

"What did you do this summer?" Mr. Greesy asked.

"My family usually goes to Wisconsin Dells for two weeks, but my older sister kind of ruined it for us this year, so I didn't really do anything except hang out with my best friends, Beth Glass and Bree Marquette," I answered, pointing at Bree. I noticed Jasmine looked at Bree funny, like she couldn't believe Bree would stoop so low as to be my best friend.

"Hanson," Mr. Greesy said, as if in deep thought, "Is your sister Eve Hanson?"

"Yes," I answered, hoping he wouldn't hold it against me.

"Well…Wisconsin Dells. That's quite a vacation. I'll bet you and your family have a great time there."

"The Barbie doll has a lot of money. What a surprise!" Jasmine exclaimed and her friends laughed along with her.

"Well, my parents work a lot and we take one vacation a year, so they like to go someplace nice." I wasn't trying to brag. I was just being honest. Besides, a lot of kids went to the Dells on vacation.

"What's your favorite thing to do in Wisconsin Dells?" Mr. Greesy asked. I wondered why he was picking on me when there were about 30 other kids in the class.

"Yeah, tell us. Did you go shopping? Enter a beauty pageant, princess?" Jasmine taunted.

I turned to her. "Why don't you just shut up?"

"What-ev-er!" Jasmine said, trying to copy my voice.

Again the class broke out in laughter, and I was so embarrassed. I sat back down and looked down at the table in front of me.

"Class! Settle down!" Mr. Greesy exclaimed.

"Are you ok?" Colin asked.

I looked away, because I was about to cry, and I didn't want him to see me. "I'm fine," I answered.

"Miss Thomas, since you seem to want the class' attention, why don't you tell us what you did this summer?" Mr. Greesy suggested.

Jasmine stood up. She wasn't even nervous or anything. She was so cool. I wished she could be my friend. She would've been so cool to hang out with. "Well, I didn't get to go to Wisconsin Dells like some snobby, rich kids. I babysat my nephew Zeke and helped my dad around the house. Oh, yeah, and I beat up my brothers," she said, then sat down.

I sat low in my seat for the rest of class and hoped this was the only class I had with Jasmine. As cool as I thought she was and as much as I wanted her to like me, she could really ruin my year, because if people heard her picking on me, they'd follow along.

At least I had Colin to look at.

Dear God, this is not going well at all. Sure, I'm sitting next to a really cute guy, but what if he decides he doesn't like me because Jasmine doesn't Please don't let that happen.

Several other kids were asked to stand and tell the class about themselves, but it never got around to Colin or Bree.

I looked over at Bree when class was about halfway over. She mouthed, "I'm sorry" to me. I just shook my head and shrugged. There wasn't anything she could have done. Nothing I expected her to do anyway.

All I could do was hope my day would get better.

Chapter 3
An Invitation

After class, Bree caught up with me. "I'm so sorry," she said.

"What are you sorry about?" I asked.

"Well, you're my friend and I should have said something to Jasmine to make her stop."

"Oh, right, and you think she would have listened to you?" I replied, shaking my head. This certainly wasn't what I had in mind when I pictured what this new school year would be like. "Don't worry about it, Bree. Don't make problems for yourself. You're the one who has to sit by her."

"That doesn't mean I should turn my back on my friends. I'll talk to her tomorrow. She's pretty cool. It's just that she doesn't know you yet."

"You sound as if you expect us to be friends," I said, and Bree just looked away, "Bree, you know that will never happen, right?"

"Why not?" she asked.

"I can't believe you're asking me this question. How do you feel about the kids that teased you last year? Do you feel like hanging out with them?"

"Emily! Why would you bring that up? I was trying really hard not to think about it and you just ruined it! Thanks a lot!"

"I'm so sorry, Brianna! Really, I am! I was just trying to make a point."

"Ok, but don't bring it up again." We hugged to seal the deal and I felt much better. It seemed I wasn't doing anything right and the first day of school was turning out to be a disaster and it practically just started!

"Hey, Emily!" I heard a guy's voice from behind me. It was Colin.

"Yes?" I quickly turned around, curious and hopeful at the same time.

"I'm meeting my friends after school in the parking lot. We're going to go over to Good Eatin'. Do you want to come?" He asked. He actually looked a little nervous.

Good Eatin' is a really cool restaurant where all the kids hang out. My mom and dad say that it is set up to look like a fifties diner. There are little juke boxes on the tables and the waitresses all wear long skirts with poodles on them. I'm thinking about getting a job there when I turn 16. My dad said he doesn't want any of us to work until after we graduate because school and getting good grades is our job. I'm pretty sure I can change his mind, though. I've already started writing my speech. It's all about being a responsible person and I threw in that I wanted to buy my own first car. He'll eat that up!

"Sure," I answered Colin, without thinking.

"Great! You'll really like my friends. I'll introduce you to everyone," Colin said, as he walked away.

"Your dad's not going to like that, Emily." Bree was right. My dad didn't want me dating until high school. Not only that, but I was supposed to baby-sit Dana after school everyday.

"I guess I'll have to tell Colin I can't go."

"That's too bad. That would have been a great way to make new friends. I'll bet Colin knows a lot of people."

"I didn't know you thought about stuff like that, Bree," I said, hoping she was becoming more like me, and less like a zombie.

"I don't, but you do. It's practically your whole world. I couldn't care less."

"Sure, Bree. Whatever you say!" I laughed.

"Seriously, I don't care!"

"I'll make a social diva out of you, just you wait."

"I doubt that!"

I just laughed. I teased Bree and Beth about it all the time. I knew they had it in them. All kids, somewhere deep inside, want to be popular. Some of us are just more honest about it.

"Beth and I have the next class together, so I'm going to go find her. I'm sorry about Colin," Brianna said.

I went to my next class in a daze. I couldn't go out with Colin after school, but that didn't change the fact that he had asked. It was only the first day of school, and I already had a potential boyfriend.

"Are you in this class?" Lauren asked, breaking my thoughts.

"Yeah," I answered. *Great,* I thought, *Now I have to put up with an hour of her babbling.*

Dear God, was that harsh?

"People, you can choose your own seat, but the seat you choose is yours for the entire school year so choose wisely." Mrs. Whitney strained her tiny voice to be heard over the roar of the class.

I chose a seat near the back of the room and Lauren sat next to me. Mrs. Whitney spent a lot of time shuffling with some papers and looking lost, so Lauren started talking. "How do you like school so far?"

"It's good and it's bad."

"What's that mean?" She looked confused.

"I met a guy named Colin. He's so cute and-," I started

Lauren cut me off mid-sentence. "You mean Colin Forrest?" she asked, wide eyed.

"Yeah. Colin Forrest."

"He IS cute!"

"Yeah, so anyway, he asked me out, sort of."

"Oh my gosh! Where are you going?" Lauren seemed so excited for me. She really was a nice person. Maybe I'd been too hard on her.

"Nowhere. I can't go. I have to baby-sit Dana after school. Plus, my dad says I can't date."

"Eve goes out with Price. Doesn't he care about that?"

"Yes, but the rule is we can't date until high school and she's in high school."

"Speaking of Price and Eve, you won't believe what I heard," Lauren whispered, as if anyone in the classroom cared.

"What?"

"My room is next to Price's and if you're real quiet you can hear everything that goes on in his room," Lauren started and looked around the room to make sure no one was listening.

"Go on!" I urged.

"They must have been kissing and stuff, because I heard Eve tell Price to stop. Then he tried to talk her into doing it with him!" Lauren sat back in her chair, obviously proud of herself.

"No way! Oh my gosh! My dad would freak!"

"So, how far have you gone with a boy?"

"Umm, well, I... I guess I haven't done anything. I let Carson Wilde kiss me on the cheek, but that's no big deal."

"I haven't even done that, so don't feel too bad. Tell me about it."

"There's this guy that goes to my church. His name is Carson Wilde. He goes to school here too. He is so cute! He's not as cute as Colin, but he's older. He's supposed to be in the seventh grade but he failed Kindergarten. Anyway, our Sunday School class went to County Zoo in Milwaukee. While we were there, he kissed me on the cheek. He might have kissed me on the lips after that, but the teacher showed up."

Lauren giggled. "Kissing boys on a Sunday School field trip? You naughty girl!"

Class started then and I decided I really liked Lauren.

"Hey," I whispered to her while Mrs. Whitney was looking the other way, "Do you know Jasmine Thomas?"

"Yeah. Stay away from her. She is bad news," Lauren whispered back, not taking her eyes off of Mrs. Whitney.

"She doesn't like me and I have first hour with her."

"You really don't want to mess with her."

"No, I really don't. Does she hate you too?"

"No."

"Because you stay away from her?"

"I can't stay away from her. She lives across the street from me."

"If I were you, I'd move." We both giggled and Mrs. Whitney told us to be quiet.

Mrs. Whitney asked a boy in the front row to stand up and introduce himself to the class. I wondered if we were going to be doing this all day long.

"My name is Roger Lopez. No autographs or pictures please." The class laughed including me. He was funny, and kind of cute.

"Roger is one of Colin's friends," Lauren told me after class.

"Oh, I wonder if he's going to Good Eatin' after school."

"Why?"

"Colin said he was meeting his friends after school and they're going there. He asked me if I wanted to go."

"Be careful, Emily. Colin's a sweetie but some of his friends are jerks."

I didn't know what to say to that so I just walked to my next class, which Lauren and I also had together.

Good morning, God. If Colin is sweet, like Lauren says, does it matter that his friends are jerks? Please don't let Colin be a jerk. Breathe. White light.

"Do you know Kenny Torn?" Lauren asked, shyly.

"No, I don't think so," I answered.

"I went to grade school with him. He's really nice and I like him. I think he might like me too. I used to let him cheat off my homework and on tests."

"Oh, Lauren! Why would you do that?"

Lauren shrugged and looked away. I got the feeling she knew it was wrong, but she didn't want to admit it. I also got the feeling she thought I would think it was cool and that made me a little mad. Cheating for a boy is just dumb.

"Not only is it wrong to cheat, but he was probably so nice to you so that you would give him answers."

"Right, because there's no way he would like me." Tears were in her eyes and I was sorry I said anything.

"Lauren, that's not what I meant and you know it. I'm sure there are plenty of guys here who like you, and maybe even Kenny does. I'm just saying that it sounds like he was using you and you deserve better than that."

"Well, Kenny isn't like that! I don't know how you can say things like that about someone you don't even know."

"Let's just drop it, ok? I don't want to fight."

"Fine. Just try to think about my feelings next time."

I made a mental note not to bring up Kenny Torn ever again. If Lauren wanted to talk about him, I would just listen and keep my opinions to myself. I had a horrible feeling she was going to get hurt, though.

"There he is!" Lauren whispered, loudly, pointing to a tall, thin guy walking on the other side of the hallway. He was cute, as Lauren had said, but there was something about him I didn't like. First of all, he looked way to old to be in middle school. Also, he had this look on his face like he thought he was something special. I really didn't like him.

Dear God, please, please, please watch over Lauren. Breathe.

No matter how hard I tried, I couldn't see the white light. This boy was trouble and I intended to ask around about him.

Meanwhile, I had to make it through this first day of school with no more drama!

Chapter 4
More Trouble

Lauren and I walked into the gymnasium, and I felt my heart sink. I'd never been too fond of gym class, but it looked as if I might have extra trouble this year. Jasmine sat on the first row of bleachers among several other girls. She was bouncing a basketball and laughing loudly. She was already dressed out. I was so glad because I wouldn't have wanted to change into my gym clothes with her around. I don't know why, but I was sure she'd find a way to torture me.

Three girls I'd gone to grade school with-Christa, Jolene, and Amanda-started squealing.

"Emily!" they exclaimed, together.

"Hey! Are you in this class?"

"I was wondering if I'd have any classes with you. How are you? I didn't get to see you all summer!" Jolene said.

"I'm good." I hugged Jolene but not the other two. I wondered if they noticed. Wondered, not cared. "This is Lauren. Lauren, this is Christa, Jolene, and Amanda. We went to grade school together," I said. I knew they wouldn't like Lauren. They were snobs.

"Aren't you Frank McCloskey's daughter?" Amanda asked and I sighed. I'd forgotten.

Amanda's dad was the morning disc jockey for Harvey's only radio station, WDDK. He had been a disc jockey in Milwaukee, but he made the wrong people mad so they moved here to get away from the city. He didn't stop doing the kind of stories that made people mad, though. He did a story on equal opportunity in the workplace and did some interviews at Rowan Plastics, where Lauren's dad works. Mr. McCloskey made some crude comments, and he and Amanda's dad became enemies.

Lauren just looked down at the floor. She was probably pretty embarrassed about her father, who I knew was a real jerk just from being at his house for Price's birthday party. He had ordered Lauren's mom around like she was his slave. Price complained about him a lot. Lauren probably felt the same way.

I felt sorry for Lauren. She seemed like the type of girl who really wanted to be liked. You know, the kind of girl who will do anything a popular person asks her to like Kenny Torn asking her to cheat for him. Now she had to face these girls, who I know only like a certain kind of person and Lauren didn't fit their description of friend material. Christa and Amanda just looked at her like she was trash. Jolene is the nicest of the three of them, but she always goes along with whatever the other two say. I had invited Jolene over to my house once, and she told me that sometimes she doesn't like Amanda and Christa, but that it was better to be their friend than their enemy. I agreed, but I also didn't think it was a good reason to be someone's friend. I prayed that she would find the strength to stand up to them.

Amanda and Christa left the locker room, but Jolene followed Lauren and I as we chose two lockers in the next aisle. Lauren seemed a little shaken by the confrontation with Amanda. It must be hard to have a dad like Frank McCloskey, who is so well known for being a bad person.

Lauren changed her clothes in silence, probably waiting for Jolene to make some sort of insulting comment about either her or her father. It didn't happen.

"Have you seen Carson?" Jolene asked.

I felt myself blush. "No. Why should I care?"

"Well, I thought you two were a 'thing'."

"I guess you didn't hear. He broke up with me," I said, facing my locker.

The three of us went back to the gymnasium and joined Amanda and Christa.

"Hey, Lauren!" Jasmine called from the bleachers. I was relieved to get her away from Amanda, but nervous about what Jasmine wanted.

"Emily, you really know how to pick the biggest losers to be friends with," Christa said.

"Lauren's ok. She's nothing like her dad," I argued.

"It's alright, Emily. We understand. It's charity!"

Good morning, God. Please forgive Christa and Amanda for being mean.

Lauren came back, her face all red.

"What was that about?" I asked.

"She wanted to know why I'm standing with you," Lauren said.

"What did you say?"

"I told her that you're my friend."

"And?"

"She said she doesn't know why I'd be friends with someone who's just going to stab me in the back."

"Why would she say that? She doesn't even know me!"

"That's what I said, but she just said that she knows your 'type'."

"Whatever! I wouldn't do that. You know that, right?"

Lauren shrugged. "I guess I don't really know you that well, either."

"You can believe what you want, Lauren, but you told me that Jasmine is trouble and now, all of a sudden, you're going to believe her over me?" I couldn't believe Jasmine was trying to turn Lauren against me. What did I do to this girl to make her so mad? It couldn't be just because I bumped into her.

"I didn't say I believe her. I just said I don't know you that well."

"Ok, fine. I'm telling you, I'm not the kind of person who goes around stabbing her friends in the back."

"Hey, you alright, Emily?" Jolene asked, smiling. She wasn't a very pretty girl, but she had a great smile and the whitest teeth I'd ever seen. Unfortunately, she didn't smile much. She was what my mom would call "melancholy".

"I'm fine. I can't seem to do anything right today, that's all," I answered.

"Things will get better. You'll see." Not only did she seem sad all the time, she also seemed much older than the rest of us.

After Coach Mills took attendance, we picked teams for volleyball. Christa was chosen to be a captain, so I was picked pretty quickly, but poor Lauren was nearly last. Jasmine was picked first for the team I wasn't on.

"Don't break a nail, blondie." Jasmine said to me, as she walked to the other side of the net.

I had assumed Lauren would be bad at sports since she was picked last, but she was awesome. I guess picking teams in gym class is more about popularity than actual ability. I made a mental note to pick Lauren first if I ever got the chance. She was more of an athlete than Jolene, Christa or even Amanda.

My team won thanks to Lauren. I think I even saw something in Christa's eyes, maybe acceptance? Probably just my wishful thinking.

I trotted over to Lauren and put my arm around her neck as we walked to the bleachers.

"Good job, girl!"

"Thanks!" Lauren replied, excitedly. "You were good, too."

"I'm ok, but we won the game because of you," I said, loudly, so Christa would hear.

Lauren and I both looked at Christa, who smiled and nodded.

"Thanks, Emily. By the way, I don't think you're going to stab me in the back," Lauren said.

"Don't be too sure!" I teased, punching her back lightly.

She elbowed me in the ribs and we both laughed. That's when I knew we would become great friends.

The most horrible thing happened when Lauren and I went to our gym lockers. In our attempt to avoid being near Amanda and Christa, Lauren and I chose lockers near Jasmine's. We hadn't known, since Jasmine was already dressed out and in the gym before we got to class.

"Look, you just need to stay out of my face. Don't look at me, don't talk to me," Jasmine said, pointing her finger so close to my face, I could have bitten it.

"Why are you being so mean to me? I apologized for bumping into you this morning. As far as I know, I haven't done anything else to make you mad," I whined.

Jasmine just looked away. She seemed so mad and I had no idea why.

I ran into Bree on my way to my 3rd hour class, which was math, my weakest subject. Bree had gym.

"I don't get it. How can Jasmine be so mad at me for bumping into her even after I said I was sorry?" I asked, not really expecting Bree to have the answer. Surprisingly, she did.

"She isn't, Emily. She isn't mad about that at all."

"Then, what is it?"

"She overheard her boyfriend and his friends talking about how cute you are."

"When?"

"In the parking lot this morning. It happened before you ran into her."

"Who's her boyfriend?"

"I don't know. She didn't say. She wasn't even talking to me. I heard her talking to her friends in Science."

How unfair! It wasn't my fault her boyfriend thought I was cute. Why did that upset her anyway? Jasmine was a very pretty girl. She didn't have any reason to worry.

I walked slowly to my math class. I hoped Jasmine wouldn't be there.

I got my wish. She wasn't there, but a couple of her friends were. I recognized them from Science class. I chose a seat as far away from them as possible.

"Hey, Emily!" It was Amanda. In spite of the way I felt about her, I was relieved to see someone I knew and there couldn't be a better someone than Amanda. She had her dad's flair for starting or ending trouble. I knew without a doubt that if one of Jasmine's tough friends picked on me, Amanda would have my back.

My theory proved correct. About halfway through class, I felt a tap on my back. A skinny, blond haired boy with dark rimmed glasses pointed at a girl sitting across the room. I knew from roll call that her name was Macy.

"You better watch your back, girl. Jasmine's not playing games with you," she said.

"Back off, goon! I don't play games either," Amanda said. The teacher had left the room and I was afraid something like this would happen.

"I'm just sayin'" Macy replied, with attitude.

I sunk in my chair. How could I have been so wrong about middle school? It was horrible and I was miserable.

"What's that all about?" Amanda asked me.

"You know Jasmine from gym class?" I asked and Amanda nodded. "Well, I guess her boyfriend said I was cute and now she hates me. I don't know what to do about it."

"That's easy. Tell her if she can't control her man, maybe she doesn't deserve him or maybe he's done with her. Why would he say something like that to her anyway?"

"She overheard him with his friends."

"Or maybe he wanted her to hear him because he wants to break up but he doesn't want to do the breaking. Typical mind tricks." Amanda said.

    I laughed. "Are you going to be a psychiatrist when you grow up?"

    "Thinkin' about it!" Amanda replied, popping her gum.

Chapter 5
Lunch

Lauren and I had lunch at the same time, so we found a table together and looked around for other friends. The cafeteria was very crowded and loud. We chose a table near the table where the middle school elite sat. I don't know how someone got to be part of that group, but I wanted to find out.

The popular kids weren't hard to find. They just had this thing about them that stood out, which is kind of weird cause that's the last thing they want. They think the whole school revolves around them and they don't notice much that goes on outside of their little circle. I know so much because my sister, Eve, had been part of that group when she was in middle school. She was most likely, now, part of the high school elite. I was a little jealous of her, but then I realized I wouldn't be able to be in that circle and still be friends with Beth and Bree, since they had no interest at all in being popular.

"I can't believe how close our schedules are! This is pretty cool, because I only had one real friend and her parents sent her to St. Jude's Catholic School this year. I was so afraid I wouldn't have any friends here," Lauren said. It was kind of weird the way she admitted things like that to me when we hardly knew each other. I guess she had the same feeling I did about us becoming really good friends.

It amazed me how she paid no attention to the cool kids. She had seemed like she would do anything to be part of that clique.

"I'm kind of glad you aren't in my 3rd hour, though," I said.

"Why? I'm not! My 3rd hour is so boring. I don't know anyone. Well, no one knows me, I should say."

"I have 3rd hour with Amanda. I'm hoping the two of you stay as far away from each other as possible. She will never get over what happened between her dad and your dad. Trust me. I know her and she doesn't let go of grudges. That's why I'm glad

I have that class with her because a couple of Jasmine's friends are in there too and one of them is pretty tough looking." I explained.

"You mean Macy."

"How did you know who I was talking about?"

"Macy is a few years older than us. She's failed three grades. Jasmine's pretty smart, so our 4th grade teacher asked her to help Macy, you know, tutor her. They've been friends ever since. They're practically family. Jasmine's sister and Macy's brother are married. They have a baby."

"Zeke."

"Yeah. Zeke. How'd you know?"

"She was talking about him in 1st hour."

"He's really a cutie!"

"You know him?"

"Yeah. They live across the street from me, remember?"

"I know Jasmine lives across the street from you, but if her sister is married…"

"She's married but they can't afford to live on their own, I guess. That happens sometimes, you know. Not everyone has a perfect life." Lauren made this last comment with so much anger in her voice. I didn't say anything after that. Apparently, it was a sore subject and I didn't want to get into it. I was grateful to see Jolene approaching us.

"Emily! Hey, can I sit with you guys?" Jolene looked relieved to see me.

"Sure. Where are Christa and Amanda?" I asked, looking around.

"They have B lunch." I knew there had to be a reason she was going to sit with us.

We didn't even eat anything. We spent the entire lunch hour talking. Lauren and Jolene really got along. They had a lot in common. They both loved sports and kept talking about baseball, which did not hold my interest. I was happy to see Lauren and Jolene getting along so well, though. I wondered if Jolene would break away from Christa and Amanda after all.

"Colin must have B lunch. I don't see him anywhere," Lauren said, obviously changing the subject to include me.

"I know and I have to tell him I can't go to Good Eatin' with him today! What am I going to do?"

"I had 3rd hour with a boy named Colin. He's pretty cute," Jolene said. "I couldn't stop staring at him. I love his eyes!"

"I know! Can you believe he asked me to go to Good Eatin' with him?"

"You are so lucky, Emily Hanson!" Jolene replied.

I smiled. Yes, I was lucky that a cute boy asked me out, but not lucky enough to get to actually go. I hoped he'd give me another chance.

"Look over there. There's Cheyenne. Could she get any weirder? I heard she has six tattoos, but you can't see them because her clothes cover them," Jolene pointed out.

"Where did you hear that? It's probably not true. Even if we can't see them, it would be hard for her to keep them from her parents," I said.

"I heard she doesn't have parents. Her father died of an overdose of Heroin and her mom lit herself on fire! Cheyenne lives with her older brother now and he doesn't care what she does," Lauren added.

I laughed. "I don't believe a word of that!"

Lauren shrugged. "I'm just telling you what I heard."

"I heard the same thing," Jolene said.

"Do you guys believe everything you hear?" I asked.

"Not everything. If I did, I would believe that you and Carson Wilde made out at the zoo last year," Jolene said, smiling.

"I did not make out with him! He kissed me, that's all. It wasn't even on the lips!" I explained.

"I believe you, but a lot of people think you did, thanks to Ryan Freeley."

"Ryan Freeley is a jerk!" I said, loud enough for him to hear me. He was sitting at the elite's table next to a popular seventh grader, PT Rommel.

He looked over at me and laughed, which made him even more of a jerk. I was surprised he acknowledged me at all since he became part of the popular group and I didn't. Apparently, you don't have to be a very good person to be part of that group. I knew very few people at that table, but the ones I did know were stuck up and mean.

Good afternoon, God. I'm sorry for being such a gossip. I guess it isn't very nice.

Chapter 6
After School

I was so upset when the end of the day came, and I still hadn't found Colin to tell him I couldn't go to Good Eatin' with him and his friends. Luckily, I found his friend, Roger.

"Roger!" I called to him.

He smiled big. "I don't know you."

"My name is Emily Hanson. I'm a friend of Colin Forrest."

"Lucky for Colin." Roger was flirting and I didn't want to flirt back, which was a first for me.

"Are you going to Good Eatin' with him?"

"Well, I wasn't going to, but if you're going...," he hinted.

"No, I can't go, but I can't find Colin to tell him, so I need you to tell him for me."

"Yeah, sure," Roger said, before he called out to one of his friends, and ran off.

Brianna and Beth were waiting outside the bus for me. "Emily! You almost missed the bus!" Beth said.

"I know. I was trying to find Colin."

"Who's Colin?" Beth asked. We didn't have a single class together, and I hadn't seen her all day, not even at lunch, so she didn't know anything about Colin or Jasmine, either, except that I had bumped into her that morning.

"Colin's the guy she sits next to in science class. He's pretty hot. I mean, he's no Dwayne Gordon, but he's ok," Bree said, without thinking.

"Aha! I knew you liked Dwayne!" Beth and I laughed. We caught Brianna finally! She never talked about boys, but I knew she thought about them. I'd just needed proof.

"I don't like him!"

"You just said he was hot!" Beth pointed out.

"Well, I do have eyes. I think he's cute, but I don't like him."

Dwayne got on the bus. Beth and I giggled. He walked by, not even noticing. "Don't embarrass me!" Brianna whispered.

Dwayne is tall and thin, but not too thin. He was wearing blue jeans and a black jacket over a white shirt.

"Will you quit staring at him?" Bree commanded more than asked.

"What do you care? You don't like him, remember?" Beth teased.

I had to be home to baby-sit Dana until my mom got home from work. I think Eve should be the one babysitting since I am just 11 years old, but somehow she got out of it. Probably because my parents don't really trust her. Whatever the reason, I couldn't go to Beth's house, which is where we like to hang out most because her parents are so cool. I invited them to my house instead. I didn't want to miss the "after the first day of school" chat.

"I can't believe Colin asked me out! I am still reeling from that one! I mean, how cute is he!" I exclaimed.

"What are you gonna do? Your dad is gonna freak out. Remember what happened last year when Jake Tamlin called you?" Bree reminded me.

I definitely remembered. My dad threw a fit. He got on the phone and told Jake to never call again and then, as if that wasn't bad enough, he talked to Jake's dad and told him not to let Jake call. Not only did Jake never call again, he never talked to me again.

"I have a couple classes with Jake. He didn't talk to me, though. I think he's afraid to," Beth said, laughing.

"Maybe you think that's funny, but I really liked him. My dad totally ruined my life."

"Oh, Emily. You're such a drama queen!" Beth said, rolling her eyes. "I'll be right back. I have to use the bathroom."

After Beth left the room, Bree bit her lip, which meant she had something to say, but she wasn't sure she wanted to say it.

"What's up?" I asked.

"Nothing. It's just…," she started.

"It's just what?"

"Nothing."

"Oh no! You can't do that. You can't hold back on me now!"

"I was just wondering if you would be mad if I was friends with Jasmine."

"Yes!" I answered, quickly. I couldn't believe what I was hearing.

"Why? I wouldn't stop being friends with you."

"I would stop being friends with you."

"There's no reason why you can't be friends with her, too."

"Uh, yes there is. She hates me and I hate her."

"How can you hate her? You barely know her." Bree gave me that look like I'm a child and she's all-knowing.

"I know enough! She makes fun of me, she looks at me like she wants to beat me up. What do you expect? Hugs and kisses?" I was so hurt. Bree was supposed to be one of my best friends. I would never have done this to her!

Our conversation was interrupted by Beth, standing in my doorway, looking white as a ghost. "Um, I have to go home now," she said.

"Why? What's wrong? Are you sick?" I asked.

"No, not really. I just started my period."

My mouth flew open and I jumped up. "Oh, my gosh, Bethany! You started your period before me, in my own house?" I was kind of mad for some reason, or maybe I was jealous.

"Focus, Emily. This isn't about you. Congratulations, Beth!" Bree said.

"Congratulations? Why? This is horrible, disgusting, and humiliating!" Beth ran out of my house and over to hers which is across the street and three houses down.

"I really didn't think she'd be the first of us to get her period, did you?" I asked Bree. We had forgotten the fight we were having about Jasmine. This was more important.

"Well, I knew it wasn't going to be me. I guess I'm not surprised she was the first. I am surprised she acted that way, though. I mean, how many times did we talk about this and we were all excited about it?"

I shrugged. "Maybe she's not ready."

"You're jealous, aren't you?" Bree shook her head. "You SO need to get over yourself."

I couldn't believe it. It was the worst day of my life. A totally cool girl hated me and Bree wanted to be friends with her. I was stuck babysitting my little sister instead of hanging out at Good Eatin' with Colin and his friends, and to top it off, Beth started her period before me. Could things really get any worse?

One good thing happened. A cute boy asked me out!!!

That night, when I climbed into bed, I prayed.

Dear God, I'm sorry for saying I hate Jasmine. I don't hate her. I just hate the things she said. I'm sorry for being mad at Bree, but she really hurt my feelings. How can she even think about being friends with Jasmine after all the mean things Jasmine said about me? Thank you for all the good things that happened today, like Colin asking me out, even though I didn't get to go. Good night, God.

Chapter 7

An Unexpected Friend

I didn't even want to see Beth and Bree the next day, but there was no way to avoid it. I walked to the bus stop, dreading the fight I knew we would have. Bree was there, but not Beth.

"Where's Beth?" I asked. I had my arms crossed to show that I was mad, but since I was carrying books, Bree probably didn't even notice.

"She's not coming to school today. She said she has cramps."

"Oh, that makes sense, I guess." I looked away then. I was jealous and a little angry about Beth starting her period, but I was really hurt by Bree. How could she want to be friends with Jasmine after what she'd said about me?

"Look, Emily, if you don't want me to be friends with Jasmine, I won't."

"That's not the point. You want to be friends with her and that hurts my feelings. I thought we were, like, best friends."

"I am your best friend. That's why I think you should try to make friends with Jasmine. You're going to have a hard time dealing with her all year if you don't. She'll make fun of you in front of Colin. Everyday, maybe."

"She doesn't want to be friends with a snobby, rich 'Barbie doll', Bree. We'll never be friends." Tears were forming in my eyes.

"Do you really think you look like a Barbie doll? I really don't think Jasmine was giving you a compliment. I think she was saying that you think you look like a Barbie doll, but you really don't."

"Are you trying to make me even more mad?"

"Why does everything have to be about you?"

"What?"

"Just like with Beth and her period, you made it all about you. You think you're better than everyone else. That's why no one likes you!" The bus pulled up as Bree was saying this and she climbed on and went all the way to the back.

"What do you mean no one likes me?" I yelled back to her. We were the only ones on the bus so far and I knew the driver was listening.

"You heard me, Emily. Everyone thinks you're a spoiled, conceited princess. Even Beth and I think so."

I hunched down in my seat and cried into my hands. I couldn't believe how mean Bree was being. She'd never said anything like that to me before.

When Dwayne Gordon got on the bus, he stopped at my seat and sat down. "You alright? What's up?" he asked.

I sucked in my breath. *God? Help! I don't know what to say!*

I'd seen Dwayne before at my grandma's church, at Priddy Park a couple of times, once at the beach by Pretty Willow Lake, on the bus the day before and a few times at school, but this was the first time he'd ever spoken to me. His eyes were so deep and mysterious. I was used to seeing him with sunglasses on, but it was a cloudy day and he didn't need them.

"I'm ok," I answered.

"Anything I can help with?" He smiled. What a smile!

"Seriously, I'm fine," I couldn't believe I was talking to a celebrity!

"My name is Dwayne," He held out his hand. He wanted to shake my hand? He was so mature for our age.

"I'm Emily. I know who you are."

"No, you don't."

"Yes, I do. You're Lefty Gordon's son. I've seen you around."

"You don't know who I am, though. You know who my dad is. Me you know nothing about." He talked so mature for our age. Maybe that's how they acted in private school.

We talked the whole way to school, which isn't very far, but it felt like it, because I was in a daze. I looked back at Bree a couple of times and she was glaring at me. I knew she was jealous and I was glad.

Good morning, God. I'm sorry for wanting to make Bree jealous.

"You like school so far?" Dwayne asked.

"It's ok. It's different than grade school," I answered.

"I used to go to private school, so it's really different for me too. At first, I was like, 'I don't want to go to public school' but then it was all 'Oh snap! I get to go to school with my gal.'"

I was wondering what lucky girl was Dwayne's girlfriend when we reached the school parking lot. When the bus door opened, there stood Jasmine and she was looking right at me.

"What's up?" Dwayne asked.

"That girl hates me," I answered, making a face.

"Oh."

I climbed down the stairs of the bus right behind Dwayne, who walked right over to Jasmine. She was standing with her hands on her hips. If looks could kill, I would be on my way to the morgue.

"Why were you sitting next to her?" she asked Dwayne.

"Jasmine, this is Emily," he said.

"I know who she is. I wanna know why you were sitting with her. Your bus isn't that crowded." Jasmine looked so mad.

"We were talking. Don't make a big deal out of nothing," Dwayne answered.

"C'mon. I have to go to my locker." Jasmine glared at me as she walked away.

"I'll talk to you later, Emily," Dwayne called back to me, and I nodded. I was still so shocked. His girlfriend was Jasmine?

"I know you did that to get back at me," Bree said, from behind me as I was watching Dwayne and Jasmine leave and wondering why someone like Dwayne could like someone like Jasmine.

"You mean talking to Dwayne? No, I didn't. He started talking to me. Was I supposed to ignore him?"

"I know you're not even interested in him."

"Maybe I am,"

"No, you're not. You just want to make me jealous."

"He's cute, he's sweet, he's smart. Yeah, you know what? I think I like him. I think I'll ask him out."

"You better not!"

"I guess you're right. He has a girlfriend. Why don't you ask your buddy, Jasmine, all about it."

Good morning, God. I'm sorry for fighting with Bree.

When I got to class, I was just in time. The bell rang as I was taking my seat. Colin was looking very unhappy. So was Jasmine. So was Bree.

Because of everything that had happened, I had forgotten all about the day before and how I hadn't been able to go out with Colin, so I was surprised when he turned to me with a very hurt look on his face.

"You know, if you didn't want to go out with me, you could've just said so instead of standing me up. I told all my friends you were coming. I felt so stupid when you didn't show up," Colin said.

"I can't help it that I had to get home. Someone has to be there to watch my little sister. What could I do?" I asked. This day was starting so badly.

"You could have told me."

"I couldn't find you, so I told Roger to tell you I couldn't make it."

"Roger?" Colin frowned.

"Yeah. Roger Lopez. I heard he was your friend."

"He is, but he didn't tell me anything about you. I didn't even know he knew you."

"He really doesn't. I have a class with him and a friend of mine told me that he was a friend of yours, so when I couldn't find you to tell you that I couldn't make it, I asked him to tell you. He didn't?"

Mr. Greesy looked up from his desk. We were supposed to be reading a chapter from our textbooks. Colin said softly, "No, he didn't."

From across the room, I could hear Jasmine talking to her friends. "She's trying to get my man, but Dwayne's not going to go out with some skinny, blond bubble head. She just better stay away from him."

"Is there something you'd like to share with the class, Miss Thomas?" Mr. Greesy asked.

"No, sir," Jasmine said aloud, then, more quietly, "I don't share."

Chapter 8
My Drama

"What's up with you today?" Lauren asked me in English class.

"I have had such a bad day, Lauren. My friends are mad at me, Jasmine thinks I'm trying to steal her boyfriend and I'm pretty sure she wants to kill me. Colin thinks I stood him up. This is the worst day of my life!"

"Wow, you really have had a bad day. So, who's Jasmine's boyfriend?"

"Lauren! I'm in total panic mode and all you can think about is gossip?" I really wasn't mad. The last thing I wanted to do was get into another fight.

"I'm sorry," Lauren apologized and added, "You know me."

"Well, get ready for this. Jasmine's boyfriend is Dwayne Gordon."

She didn't disappoint me. Her eyes flew open and I thought she was going to faint. "Dwayne Gordon? THE Dwayne Gordon? 2nd baseman for the Harvey Dodger Boys?"

"He plays baseball? I didn't know that." The Harvey Dodger Boys are the local sports teams that boys our age play on. The high school team is the Harvey Dodgers. I'd never gone to a game, so I didn't know Dwayne played ball like his dad.

"He's the star of the team. People say he'll probably play professionally like Lefty, except he'll be a position player instead of a pitcher," Lauren explained.

I didn't really know what that meant, so I didn't respond. Roger was passing a letter to the girl sitting next to him and he pointed to me. I squirmed in my seat, because I was sure Mrs. Whitney would see the note.

"Hey, Pretty Girl," it read.

I looked over at Roger. He was smiling at me. I cleared my throat and wrote on the same piece of paper, "Hey yourself. I'm mad at you." I folded the note and passed it back the way it was passed to me.

He read it, looked at me and frowned, wrote something and passed it back.

"What did I do?" it read.

"It's what you didn't do. You never told Colin that I couldn't go to Good Eatin' yesterday. He's mad at me," I wrote.

"Why do you care? You don't really like him, do you?" he wrote.

"I like what I know," I wrote.

"Do you like what you know about me?" he wrote.

"No. I told you I'm mad at you," I wrote.

When Roger read this, he scoffed and raised his hand.

"What is it, Roger?" Mrs. Whitney asked.

"Emily keeps writing me notes. I can't concentrate on the assignment," Roger said, innocently.

"Emily, I'll see you after class."

Lauren leaned over and whispered, "Like I said, some of Colin's friends are jerks."

After class, Mrs. Whitney gave me an extra assignment and a lecture about conduct in the classroom.

God, are you punishing me? What did I do?

Lauren waited for me after school. Her last class was right across the hall from mine. "I forgot to tell you, I met Carson Wilde. I sit next to him in Pre-Algebra."

"You didn't say anything about me, did you?"

"Of course I did!"

"Oh my gosh, Lauren, how embarrassing!" I covered my face.

Lauren laughed. "I didn't say anything about what you told me yesterday. He asked me if I had any friends he might know. I mentioned you, because you both went to Cordelia A. P. Harvey."

"So, what did he say?"

"You should have seen the smile on his face! He didn't say anything except that he knew you, but I could tell that he likes you."

"He doesn't like me anymore, Lauren. Don't tell me stuff like that."

"I'm telling you, he still likes you."

"I don't care. He might have lied to Ryan about what happened last year at the zoo. He probably wanted his friends to think he was cool, so he made up a story about me."

"You don't know that for sure. Maybe Ryan lied."

"Maybe. I'll see you tomorrow," I said, and left her at her bus.

Dwayne was waiting outside our bus.

"Hey Emily. Sorry about this morning. Jasmine's not usually like that."

I laughed and without thinking, I said, "Really? You're trying to tell me she's not always mean?"

"You don't even know her, Emily." Dwayne looked a little mad.

"I don't mean to make you mad by saying that. I just don't like her. I know she's your girlfriend, but I can't like her just because you were nice to me this morning. If I had known that Jasmine was your girlfriend, I never would have talked to you. As if I didn't have enough problems with her, now she thinks I'm trying to steal her boyfriend. Thanks a lot, Dwayne." I climbed onto the bus and sat down with a guy I'd gone to grade school with. I started talking to him right away so that Dwayne would know I had nothing more to say to him. He was a celebrity and I felt lucky that he even noticed me, but I'd had such a bad day and I was in no mood to be nice to him just because his dad is famous.

When Bree and I got off the bus together, I sensed that we were going to have another fight. I just wanted to go home.

"So, now you're too good to talk to Dwayne?" Bree asked.

"I didn't say I was too good! I just didn't want to talk to him. It's none of your business anyway! You're nothing to Dwayne."

"Jasmine is my friend and you're trying to steal her boyfriend."

"That's messed up, Bree, and you know it. You have some serious issues," I replied, and walked home.

I had so much to think about. I was excited about Colin, but if Carson really still liked me, that would be pretty cool, too. They were both really cute and sweet.

"Great! You're home! I need to get back to the office, but Dana is really sick. I took her to the doctor today and he gave her some medicine. I wrote the instructions down on a piece of paper on the dining room table. She's resting right now. She's been vomiting and she has diarrhea," my mom announced as I walked in the door. She threw her suit jacket on and was gone quicker than I could say "Hello". Vomiting and diarrhea. Great. The perfect ending to the perfect day.

Dear God, I really want to do the right thing but I don't know what to do. Could you, please, send me a sign?

Chapter 9
The Truce

At the end of the week, things still weren't any better with Bree, Jasmine, or Colin. Roger was becoming a problem too. He had a bad habit of pushing me, pulling my hair or making fun of me in some other way. He was playing childish games, and I knew it was because he likes me and I like Colin.

Beth still hadn't come back to school, so Bree and I decided to do something about that. We called a truce long enough to convince Beth to come back to school.

"Hi Mrs. Glass," Bree and I said when she answered the door.

"Hi girls! Come on in. I hope you two can put some sense into my daughter's head."

Yeah, we miss her at school," Bree answered Mrs. Glass and turned to me, "Can I go in alone first?"

"Sure. I guess so."

"I haven't had a chance to talk to you since school started. How is everything, Emily?" Mrs. Glass asked, folding laundry.

"I don't know. Parts of it are really great, and then there's Jasmine," I said, as I picked up a towel to fold.

"Who's Jasmine?"

"She's this girl that hates me. She goes out with Dwayne Gordon. She thinks I'm trying to take him away from her."

"Are you? I mean, I've heard you guys talking about how hot he is. Hot and cool and gorgeous."

"and rich and famous. Don't forget rich and famous!" I added and we laughed together. I wished for the millionth time in my life that my mom could be so cool.

"So how is the boy situation at school? Whenever I ask Beth things like that she rolls her eyes at me."

"Well, there's this boy named Colin. I sit next to him in Science. He's really cute and I like him a lot. He asked me out on the first day of school, but I couldn't go, because you know how my dad is. I had to baby-sit anyway. Now Colin's mad at me."

"He's mad because you couldn't go out with him. That's not very fair."

"Well, that's not the whole story. It's a big mess. I just wish he'd get over it."

"I'm sure it will work out."

"Um, Mrs. Glass, can I talk to you?"

"Of course you can."

"So much is going wrong and I feel like God is punishing me," I blurted out.

"Oh, Emily, you know better than that! That's not how God works. God loves you. He loves us all."

"Then why are all these bad things happening?"

"Everything happens for a reason. I don't mean to sound corny, but it's true. Something good will come from this, even if it's just a life lesson. Try to find the good in everything. I'm sure if you think about everything bad that's happened, something good has too…or it will."

Bree came out of Beth's room and dragged me in by the arm. "She won't listen to me."

"What's up, Beth? When are you coming back to school?" I asked.

"I'm not ever going back to school. People make fun of me enough for being fat. Everyone will know what happened and they'll make fun of me more," Beth pouted.

"No one's going to make fun of you for having your period. Every girl gets her period sooner or later," I said.

"Well, I would rather have mine later."

"I don't get it. We've talked about this for a couple years now and we've all been really excited about it. How come all of a sudden, you don't want to have your period?" I asked.

"You don't understand. It's gross. It smells. These stupid pads are bulky and uncomfortable, and you get cramps!" Beth yelled.

"You knew you would get cramps," Bree reminded.

"They really hurt!" Beth covered her face with her pillow.

"And people call me a drama queen? You're being ridiculous! Getting your period is the most special thing that happens to girls our age. I can't believe you started before me. You are such a baby!" I was irritated with Beth. She didn't know how lucky she was.

"That really is all you care about isn't it, Emily? You're the one who's being ridiculous. Jasmine is so right about you," Bree said, giving me that evil look again.

"That is not all I care about. I care about Beth. She needs to get over herself and come back to school before she gets so far behind, she can't catch up."

"What's going on with you two?" Beth came out from under her pillow. She hates fights, especially between the three of us.

"Emily can't shut up about how you started your period before her. That's all she cares about. She's jealous and she can't stand it. She can't stand not being first."

"That's not true, Brianna. What is your problem? It's not even about this anymore, is it? This is about Dwayne. You're the one who's jealous. You're jealous because he talks to me."

"Dwayne Gordon talks to you?" Beth asked.

"Yes. He sits next to me on the bus, but he moves before we get to school because his girlfriend hates me."

"Who's his girlfriend?" Beth was starting to sound like her old self again.

"You remember that girl I ran into on the first day of school? Her name is

Jasmine. She goes out with Dwayne. I can't stand her, but Bree likes her," I said, making a face at Bree.

"Wow, I'm missing everything!"

"So does that mean you're coming back?" Bree and I asked.

Beth looked away and said, "I guess I have to go back sometime. I'll go back to school Monday," she started, "but only if you two make up. I don't want to be around you guys when you're fighting."

I looked at Bree. I was ready to be friends with her again. Fighting with her was one thing that was making my life miserable. "I can do that," I said, and opened up my arms to hug Bree.

"Ok," Bree said, and accepted my hug. "Do you swear that Dwayne is just your friend?"

"I swear. I like Colin and only Colin," I answered, even though it wasn't the truth. I didn't want to tell them about Carson yet.

Chapter 10
Sister Talk

When I got home that night, my mom was in a really bad mood. She said she'd had a bad day at work and dad wasn't helping. All through dinner they glared at each other and my mom slammed things down on the table. They were getting on my nerves.

Please, God, help my mom and dad make up.

Price was grounded for some reason, so that left Eve open for some sister time. I hoped she was in the mood for it. Sometimes she can be so sweet and we talk and laugh. Other times she is mean and doesn't want to have anything to do with me.

"Eve, can I ask you something?" I asked, cautiously. I really didn't want her to start calling me names like 'twerp' or 'brat'.

"Sure," She said, brushing her hair. She was sitting at her vanity.

"Is your period gross?"

Eve laughed. "No, it's not gross. Where did you get that idea?"

"Beth."

"Beth started her period?" She looked surprised.

"Yes! She started before me. Can you believe it?"

"Drives you crazy, doesn't it?" Eve knew me pretty well.

"I thought I would start first. I mean, I act more like a woman than she does. I'll really freak if Bree starts before me."

"Don't think so much about it. I didn't start until I was thirteen. My friend KC hasn't started yet and she's fifteen. You don't have to worry about it until you are sixteen, at least that's what my health teacher said. It doesn't mean you're still a child. A period doesn't necessarily make you a woman, anyway."

"It's part of being a woman, though."

"That's true, but it isn't the most important part. You don't have a period yet. So what? It just means you can't get pregnant. You're not having sex yet, anyway."

That reminded me of what Lauren had told me on the first day of school. "Has Price asked you to go all the way yet?" I played dumb for Lauren's sake.

"Well, yes, but I haven't, so don't go telling dad." She looked worried.

"I won't tell anyone. I promise. So, what did you tell him?"

"I told him maybe."

"Maybe? Are you kidding? You can't do that!"

"Why not? It's my body, my life," Eve looked at me in the mirror and saw how shocked I was. "Emily, has some guy asked you to…"

"No!"

"Pretty soon someone will and you should tell him 'no'."

"You just said that you might do it with Price."

"I'm way more mature than you are, Em. You should definitely wait," Eve said, putting on some huge, gawdy hoop earrings.

"So, periods really aren't gross?" I felt like she was going to start being mean so I changed the subject.

"No. You get used to it after awhile and you don't even notice it." She put a ponytail in her hair.

The phone rang and Eve answered it. "It's for you, Em," she said and handed me her purple cordless phone.

"Hello," I said, expecting it to be Beth, Bree or Lauren.

"Hi Emily. It's Colin."

"Colin? How did you get my phone number?" My heart started to beat really fast.

"I looked it up in the phone book. I called two other numbers before I got the right one. You're not mad are you?"

"No, I'm not mad, but I thought you were still mad at me."

"Roger told me what really happened. I was stupid to believe him over you. I think he likes you."

"I kind of thought Roger would deny it. I know he likes me. He flirted with me and I blew him off. He's been mean to me ever since."

"That sounds like Roger."

"So, What's up?"

"Emily, um…will you go to the mall with me tomorrow?" It was so cute the way he sounded nervous.

"Sure, I can go to the mall tomorrow. I'll meet you there at 2:00. Is that ok?" I couldn't believe how fast my heart was beating.

"Great. I'll see you then." We hung up and I did a little dance. Dana saw me and she laughed. "Eve! Guess what!"

"What?"

"Colin just asked me to go to the mall tomorrow."

"What about Dad?" I hadn't thought of that.

"I'm just going to the mall. I don't have to tell Dad I'm meeting a boy."

"Dad has a way of finding things out, Emily. Be careful." She knew what she was talking about. Eve was always getting into trouble. My dad said that every gray hair on his head has Eve's name on it.

"I will. It's really no big deal."

"So which one are you going to?" Eve started going through the clothes in her closet.

"Huh?" I asked, in a daze over Colin's call.

"Which mall are you going to?"

"Oh great! What am I going to tell Dad? There is no way he's going to drive me to a mall across town when there's one in walking distance."

"Not to mention he hates that part of town. You know what he'll say. 'God only knows what kind of people go to that mall'," Eve said, mimicking our dad.

"You have to help me, Eve. I can't cancel on Colin. He'll never ask me out again!" I started to cry. It doesn't take a lot to make me cry.

Eve sighed. "Alright. Price isn't grounded tomorrow. I'll ask him if his parents can take us to the mall. We can tell dad I'm just going over to Price's house and you're coming with me to see Lauren."

I squealed with delight. "Thank you! Thank you!" Maybe my parents weren't cool like Beth's, but I had a sneaky, cool sister!

Please don't be mad at me, God.

Chapter 11
Harvey Mall

Lauren and Price's dad dropped us off at the entrance to Harvey Mall. It was the first time I'd ever been there. Lauren came too. I was kind of glad. I didn't really want Colin to know that I didn't know my way around this mall. The last thing I wanted was to come off like I was too good to shop there. My parents were the snobs, not me.

"I can't believe you've lived here all your life and you've never been to the mall. Especially you. You are so into shopping," Lauren said, after we ditched Price and Eve.

"I usually go to The Shoppe." "The Shoppe" was the name of the mall near my house.

"Oh."

"Really, it's not that much different. It has a lot of the same stores," I lied.

"Yeah?" Lauren seemed to perk up then. I knew she was jealous of me. It made me feel kind of good.

Is that wrong?

We found Colin at an arcade called "Gamez". The Shoppe didn't have an arcade.

Lights and sounds filled the air and it was packed with kids our age and some a little older.

"Hey Emily," Colin said.

"Hi Colin. This is my friend Lauren."

"Yeah, I know Lauren. How's it going?"

"Great! So, who else is here?" Lauren craned her neck to see the whole room.

"Most of the team came."

"Oh my gosh! You mean all the Dodger Boys are here?" Lauren was acting like she'd been eating sugar all day.

I didn't know Colin was a Dodger Boy. I guessed that meant Dwayne was there and maybe Jasmine.

"Most of them are. Kenny is over there. PT is playing skee ball. Roger and Dwayne are playing air hockey. Josh is picking out a stuffed animal he just won and Travis is, of course, doing whatever his girlfriend wants," Colin said. I wondered if a lot of girls acted the way Lauren was acting and if Colin expected me to be that way.

"You never told me you play for the Dodger Boys," I said, watching Lauren as she went to flirt with Kenny Torn.

"I play first base and bat third, right in front of Dwayne."

"I don't know what that means. I don't watch baseball."

"Not even the Brewers?" Colin asked, surprised.

"I've been to Miller Park a couple of times, but I didn't really watch the game. I would like to see you play, though. Maybe I should come to one of your games."

"That would be awesome! I've never had a girl cheering me on before. Most girls that come to the game are there to see Dwayne or Roger." I wrinkled my nose when he said Roger's name, and Colin apologized.

"You may not like him, but he has a lot of fans." He leaned in real close and whispered in my ear, "I don't know why. He isn't even very good. We're both on the ski team and he's pretty good at that, but when it comes to baseball, I don't know, he just acts like he's afraid of the ball. Maybe that's why he has so many fans. They must feel sorry for him!"

I laughed and Colin pulled me into the picture booth. We made crazy faces and the pictures came out ridiculous, but I carefully slipped them into my purse. I planned on putting them in a safe place when I got home.

I felt a tap on my shoulder while watching Colin playing some video game. I turned around and was face to face with Dwayne.

"What's up?" he asked.

"Just hanging out. What about you? Where's Jasmine?" I asked, coolly.

"Babysitting her nephew."

"You guys know each other?" Colin asked, letting his game end.

"We ride the bus together. Hey, I'll see you later, alright?" Dwayne said, and walked away.

"Are you and Dwayne more than friends?"

"No! Geez, everyone keeps asking me that. Jasmine thinks I'm trying to steal him from her. Bree thinks I like him. Even Beth's mom asked."

"Sorry. I didn't mean to make you mad. I was just wondering."

"I wouldn't be here with you, Colin, if I liked someone else," I lied. I still wasn't sure about Carson.

Colin smiled and we started having fun again. I didn't see Lauren very much, but when I did see her, she was with Kenny. I wondered what the story was there.

I could hardly believe it when Eve walked in and told me we had to go. I was having so much fun. I didn't want to leave, but Eve said Mr. McCloskey was probably already waiting outside. I said goodbye to Colin, waved to Dwayne, and walked out, pretending not to notice Roger and his dirty looks.

"I had so much fun, Em. I think Kenny Torn might like me," Lauren said, excitedly, in the back of her parents' minivan.

"Really?" I doubted it.

"So? Tell me!"

"Tell you what?" I asked, acting like I had no idea what she was talking about.

"About Colin!" Lauren answered loudly and Mr. McCloskey looked at us in his rear view mirror. Lauren lowered her voice. "What happened?"

"Nothing happened. We just had a great time. Oh, we took some pictures," I said, digging for them in my purse.

"How cute!"

Mr. McCloskey pulled up in front of our house, Eve and I thanked him and climbed out of the van. Dad was waiting for us at the door, fire coming from his eyes.

"I just got off the phone with Celia McCloskey. You two girls were never there tonight. She said her husband was picking you up from the mall, from Harvey Mall!" my dad shouted.

"Yes, Daddy. We were at Harvey Mall getting tattoos on our butts and our tongues pierced. We joined a gang, bought some drugs and spray painted our names on the side of the building," Eve remarked, grinning. Another gray hair on daddy's head.

"Don't get smart with me, little girl!" he replied, pointing at Eve. Then he looked at me. "Not you too, Emily. You are both grounded until further notice."

Later that night, I knocked softly on Eve's door. It was past midnight and we had to get up early for church the next morning, but I couldn't sleep.

"What do you want?" Eve asked. She was mad. I could always tell when she was mad.

"Can I talk to you?" I didn't get an answer. "Please?" I begged.

She opened her door to let me in and I sat on the side of her bed as she climbed in under the covers. "I'm really sorry about tonight," I said.

"Yeah, so am I! I'm grounded. Do you know what that means? I won't be able to go to the party at Priddy Park after the big game. Thanks a lot, Emily!"

"I'm really sorry, Eve. I didn't think we would get in any trouble."

"I know. I'm not really mad at you. I'm just disappointed. I mean, how many times does this happen and I'm going to miss it!"

She was talking about the football game between the Dodgers and the Gateway Grizzlies, who come all the way from St. Louis every year, because the coach of the

Grizzlies and the coach of the Dodgers are brothers. They always play the Sunday after Halloween. It's really a special event and there was going to be a party at Priddy Park that night. The middle school kids were planning to have a party there on Halloween, which was on a Saturday this year. Two police officers and a teacher offered to chaperone.

"I'm going to miss my party, too," I reminded her.

"That doesn't make me happy, Emily. I don't want you to miss your party. I wish there was some way to get out of this."

"It's more than a month away, Eve. Do you really think we'll be grounded that long?"

"Oh yeah! That's what 'until further notice' means. We're going to be grounded for a long time." Eve rolled her eyes.

I decided I didn't like being bad. It wasn't worth the punishment.

The next morning before we left for church, Eve pulled me into her room. "I have an idea. Like you said, the parties are more than a month away. Let's be real sweet to dad even when he's being a jerk, and then, like, a couple days before Halloween, let's try to get him to let us go." Eve looked hopeful.

I was less hopeful and not really happy about Eve calling our dad a "jerk". He was just being a dad. "When does Dad ever fall for the sweet, innocent act?" I asked.

"He's a father. They all do. How do you think Dana gets everything she wants?"

I thought about it all through church. It wasn't the best plan, but it was the only chance we had. A month of being sweet and innocent? I could do that.

Chapter 12
Beth's Mom

"Emily, sweetheart, could you run this over to the Glass' house? I don't want to leave Dana," my mom asked, after dinner.

"You run that over, then you come right home. You're grounded, don't forget," my dad said, sternly.

I grabbed the casserole from my mom and headed out the door. As I was grabbing my jacket, I ran into Eve.

"Where are you going?" she asked.

"To Beth's house to drop this off," I answered.

She scoffed. "I knew they'd let you go out. You're their little angel."

"I'm not going to have fun. I'm just supposed to drop this off and come home. Dad said that I can't stay there."

"Whatever."

I sighed and rolled my eyes. I remembered what she'd said to me the day Colin had called me. She'd said, "I'm way more mature than you are, Em." She wasn't acting very mature.

Mrs. Glass answered the door like she was expecting me. "Hello, Emily, come on in."

"I can't stay. I'm grounded."

"I know you are, but I'd really like to talk to you. If you get into trouble, have your mom call me and I'll tell her I asked you to stay."

"What do you want to talk to me about? Isn't Beth home?" I asked, looking around.

"She went with her dad to Milwaukee today to see her grandmother. I thought she told you." Mary frowned.

"Oh, yeah, she did. There's so much going on right now. I forgot."

"I understand you girls are fighting a little."

"Not Beth and I. It's really about Bree and me."

"Well, Beth is upset about it. I hate seeing her unhappy. You girls have been friends for so long. Is it about boys?"

"Kind of. It's about Dwayne. He's my friend and Bree is jealous. She's friends with Dwayne's girlfriend, who thinks I'm trying to steal him from her. She hates me and it hurts my feelings that Brianna wants to be friends with her. Bree is trying to turn it all around so that I come off looking like a bad person and I'm not."

"No, of course you're not. This will all blow over," Mrs. Glass assured me, patting me on the shoulder.

"I know. I mean, it sort of already has. Beth made us promise to stop fighting or else she wouldn't come back to school."

Mrs. Glass laughed. "That's my girl!"

I got up to leave, but then sat back down. "Mrs. Glass, can I talk to you about something?"

"You don't have to keep asking, Emily. You can talk to me anytime."

"Eve said that someone would probably ask me to do it with them soon, and I'm not sure what to say when they do."

"Oh, sweetie, that is a subject I'd hoped to tackle much later but, unfortunately, Eve is probably right. I think you know what you should say. You should not be having sex at your age and Eve should not be having sex at her age."

"You mean because it's a sin?" I asked. We had talked about it in Sunday School.

Mrs. Glass paused. "Uhh...yes, it's a sin to have sex outside of marriage, but that's not the only reason to stay a virgin until your married. Has a boy been pressuring you for sex?"

"No, I've just been thinking about it a lot. Do you go to Hell if you have sex with your boyfriend?"

"You certainly would not go to Hell for it! Emily, you will make mistakes. Everyone does. It's important that you don't keep beating yourself up for making a mistake. The biggest mistake you can make is not learning from your mistakes."

"Thanks, Mrs. Glass. I better get home." I turned to walk home, still full of questions.

"Emily," Mrs. Glass said and I turned back to her. "I know that telling you that you shouldn't have sex isn't enough. You want to know why and I'll tell you why. Sex can be very dangerous and, at this point, it could change the course of your entire life. You could get a disease or you could get pregnant," Mary started. She paused for a moment and sighed, "A very important lesson I learned, is that sex can make things very difficult and complicated. The first time I had sex, the boy didn't want to have anything to do with me afterwards. He broke my heart. I had never felt pain like that until then. I'd broken up with boyfriends before, but I had sex with this one. It hurt so much worse, because I had given something so precious to him and he discarded it. After that, my godmother told me, and I'll never forget, women's hearts are directly connected to their vaginas and for men, most of the time, it's just about sex. At least that's true for teenaged boys. They are just bodies full of hormones."

"So, I can't trust guys?"

"I didn't say that, but if you find a guy you can trust, he'll respect your wishes when you say you aren't ready. If some guy tries to talk you into doing something that you don't want to do, he isn't worth your time and certainly not worth the pain of a broken heart."

"Thanks Mrs. Glass," I said. "Please don't tell my mom about this."

"I won't, but you should talk to her about it."

"She wouldn't understand. She would just freak out."

"She might surprise you," Mrs. Glass said, as I was leaving.

I left Beth's house feeling much better about things. I wondered if Colin was a guy I could trust.

God, I am so confused. I don't even know where to start to pray. Please watch over me and don't let me make mistakes.

Chapter 13
Boys!

Monday morning, Beth and Bree seemed excited to see me. "What happened to you Saturday night? I heard my mom on the phone. Your mom was so mad, I could hear her all the way across the room!" Beth exaggerated.

"Oh, it was nothing. My parents made a big deal about it, but it really was nothing."

Bree sighed. "You know you're going to tell us, so it might as well be now."

"Ok, ok. Eve and I told my parents that we were going over to Lauren's house and instead we went to Harvey Mall so I could meet Colin. He was there with the rest of the Dodger Boys."

Beth and Bree both opened their mouths wide and looked at each other. "Oh my gosh, Emily, your dad hates Harvey Mall!" Bree exclaimed.

"Well, see, that's what I don't get. There's nothing wrong with Harvey Mall. There were no fights, no robberies, no rapes, or any of the other things my dad is always talking about. It was just a bunch of people shopping," I said.

"She's right. My mom and I shop there sometimes," Beth agreed.

"My dad's just being stuck up as usual and now I'm grounded," I said, pouting.

"For how long?" Beth asked.

"He said, 'Until further notice'. Eve said that means a long time."

"Are you going to miss the Halloween party?" Bree asked.

"I hope not. Eve and I have a plan. We're going to be really sweet to my dad and hope he changes his mind before then."

The bus pulled up and we took our regular seats. I couldn't wait to see Dwayne. I thought Colin might have told him something about me after I left the mall on Saturday.

"Hey, Emily, was Dwayne at the mall Saturday?" Bree asked.

"Yeah, he was there," I replied.

"Oh," Bree said, looking down. She looked truly upset over him.

"Bree," I started and she looked up, "he was there alone." I smiled.

She smiled back at me. I was so glad we made up. I couldn't imagine not being friends with her or Beth. It seemed a little weird to me, though, that Bree wanted to be friends with Dwayne's girlfriend. I could never be nice to Colin's girlfriend, if he had one.

Dwayne got on the bus and sat next to me. I heard Beth suck in her breath and I remembered it was her first day back to school after starting her period. I hadn't gotten the chance to introduce her to Dwayne. Bree hadn't met him, either, because she had been sitting in the back of the bus to avoid me.

"Dwayne, these are my best friends, Beth and Bree," I said.

He turned around in his seat and smiled at them. They looked like they were ready to faint. "Hi Beth and Bree. I'm Dwayne," he said.

"Hi," they both said, real shy-like.

"So?" I asked, excitedly. "Did Colin say anything about me after I left?"

"Emily, you know I can't tell you. I can't do that to my boy," Dwayne said, sporting a huge grin.

"Yeah, ok. Can you, at least, tell me if it was good or bad?"

"He said that you looked as ugly as a badger's butt."

My heart sank and I could feel the tears coming before I noticed that Dwayne was having trouble keeping himself from laughing.

"Dwayne! He said no such thing!" I exclaimed, slapping his arm repeatedly while he laughed hysterically. Beth and Bree were both giving me a look as if to say, "You dare hit Dwayne Gordon?".

"Seriously, Emily, I didn't talk to Colin after you left." Dwayne said, after he calmed down.

I was excited about seeing Colin in first hour. We'd had so much fun at the mall. I fidgeted in my seat waiting for the bell to ring. Colin hadn't come in yet. I watched the door, excitedly. Jasmine came in looking like she was ready for a photo shoot.

"Emily?" she asked.

"What?" I asked, kind of angrily. I was getting ready for her usual insults.

"Dwayne said he saw you at the mall Saturday night."

"So? I wasn't there with him. Are you gonna tell me not to go to the mall now?"

"No, I was gonna say 'I'm sorry' so you can drop the attitude."

"What are you sorry for?"

"Dwayne said you were there with Colin and it looked like a date. I'm sorry I thought you liked Dwayne." I wondered if Dwayne had put her up to this.

"No problem."

She didn't say anything more. She went to her seat and started talking to Bree. I'm pretty sure they had become friends while Bree and I were fighting. I didn't really care, though. As long as Jasmine didn't turn Bree against me, it was none of my business if they were friends.

Colin finally came in and sat down just as the final bell was ringing. He didn't even look my way. I said hello to him, but he didn't respond. In fact, he didn't say a word to me all during class. By the time class was dismissed, I was confused.

"Colin, what's wrong? Why won't you talk to me?"

He looked at me for the first time and said, "This is school, Emily. I was paying attention to the teacher."

I was totally confused. I could feel a huge lump in my throat.

Bree caught up with me in the hall. Jasmine was with her. "Why are you walking so fast?" Bree asked.

"I don't get it! Colin ignored me all through class and now he's being kind of mean. I don't know what I did."

"Boys and men, they're all dogs," Jasmine said, "That's what my sister says, anyway."

"I don't get it," I said, "Maybe he is a jerk. Maybe I was wrong."

"Maybe he's just having a bad day, Emily. Give him a break," Bree suggested.

"I don't know," I replied, "Maybe."

Bree left Jasmine and I standing together in the hall. I never expected that to happen.

"Jasmine, why are you standing with me? I thought you hated me." I decided to just come right out and ask her what was up.

"Dwayne is my boyfriend and Bree is my friend. They both told me that I would like you if I knew you, so here I am getting to know you," she explained, "Besides, I didn't really hate you. At first, I was just having fun teasing you, but then I saw you with Dwayne and I thought you were trying to steal him from me."

"Just because I was talking to him?" I asked.

"You don't get it, do you? Dwayne is a star in this town. Girls are always after him. Even some high school girls try to talk to him."

"That must suck," I said, not really understanding her pain, but happy she was trying to be friends with me. I really did think she was cool.

"It's pretty bad when you have to worry about losing your boyfriend constantly. It doesn't help that his step-mom doesn't like me."

"Oh, I didn't know his parents were divorced." Who would be dumb enough to leave Lefty Gordon?

"Whose parents aren't divorced?" Jasmine asked. By the tone of her voice, I could tell this was a touchy subject, so I didn't tell her that my parents were still together.

"Are you and Dwayne going to the party?" I didn't have to say what party. There was only one party that everyone was talking about.

"I guess we are. Are you going?" Jasmine asked.

"I'm grounded and I was hoping to get out of it before then, but since Colin is acting this way, I don't think I'm going to bother."

"You know, Emily, you should give him another chance. I've known him for a long time. We're not friends or anything, but he's always seemed pretty cool," Jasmine said, as we split up to go to our classes.

Lauren was already in class and sitting in her seat when I got there. "So you really got into a lot of trouble for Saturday night, huh?" she asked. She already knew the answer. Her mom probably told her my dad was mad.

"Yeah, I got grounded. It wasn't even worth it. Colin's being a real jerk."

"Colin's being a jerk?" Lauren looked shocked.

"He won't even tell me why," I answered, as Roger walked into the room.

"So, Emily," he said, sitting down in the empty chair in front of my desk. He sat in it backwards, facing me and crossed his arms on my desk, "how is Colin? Is he your boyfriend? Did you let him kiss you?"

"What are you talking about, Roger?"

"I was just wondering how things were going after the big date on Saturday night. I hear he won't even look at you now. Why is that, Emily? Were you a bad girl?" Roger teased.

"No, I wasn't and don't start any rumors, Roger!"

"Or you'll what?" He was pushing me and it was working. I was mad. I was hurt. I was embarrassed.

I told Mrs. Whitney that I was sick and she gave me a note to go to the nurse's office. I didn't even make it there. I threw up in the restroom down the hall from my class.

The nurse called my dad and he came to pick me up.

"You alright, Emmy Lou?" 'Emmy Lou' is his pet name for me. He is the only person in the world that calls me that, and I love it.

"No," I answered and started crying. I didn't tell him why. I just let him believe I was sick. If I told him I was upset over a boy, he would turn the car around and make me go back to school.

"It's ok, sweetheart. I'll get you home and you can go to bed. Later, if you feel up to it, we can watch some movies together."

"Great," I said, and smiled a little. Jasmine's sister was wrong. Not all boys and men are dogs. Not my daddy.

Later that day, after I took a nap, I was feeling better. I thought about it, and I decided not to cry over Colin anymore. If he didn't want to go out with me, someone else would. Maybe Carson, or maybe someone else. There are a lot of boys at Harvey Middle School. Why should I waste my time on Colin?

"You feeling better, pumpkin?" My dad asked, opening my door.

"A little bit. My stomach still feels kinda funny," I replied, not ready to go back to school just yet.

"Does it feel too funny for ice cream?" He wiggled his eyebrows up and down.

I laughed. "I could eat some ice cream."

While we ate our ice cream, I asked my dad why he was acting weird.

"Am I acting weird?"

"Well, yeah. After what happened Saturday, I thought you'd be mad at me for a long time."

"I'm not mad at you, Emmy Lou. I never was, really. I was scared. You know how I feel about that mall and that part of town."

"It's not so bad. Just because they don't have as much money as we do, doesn't mean they're bad people. Now that I go to middle school, I know a lot of people from that part of town. There's nothing wrong with them."

"You can't understand, Emily. I am the father of three beautiful girls. It's my job to overreact."

I giggled, embarrassed by the 'beautiful' comment. "So, now, why are you acting weird?"

"I want to be more than your father, Emmy Lou. I want to be your friend. Somewhere I messed up with Eve. We're like enemies most of the time. I can't open my mouth to speak to her without her turning it into an argument. I don't want it to be like that with you. I want you to know that you can come to me whenever you need someone," he said, then wrinkled his nose, "Except with all that woman stuff. You can talk to your mom about that."

I laughed at him and we finished our ice cream, then I went to bed and thought about everything that was going on in my life.

Can fathers and daughters be friends? Why is Jasmine being so nice to me? Why is Colin being a jerk? Why is Roger being so…Rogery? Should I find Carson and talk to him? Are all boys and men just dogs, like Jasmine said?

Chapter 14
Bree's news

After school, Beth and Bree came over to make sure I was alright. My dad said they could stay for a little while, but not too long.

"What happened?" Beth asked. "Did you get your period, too?" She looked hopeful.

"I wish! I got sick at school," I answered.

"You weren't sick this morning," Bree pointed out.

"Well, some stuff happened at school this morning," I started. They waited for me to tell them what happened, but I was afraid my dad might hear. "You have to promise not to say anything," I whispered.

"To who?" Beth whispered back.

"Don't say anything loud right now. I don't want my dad to hear anything."

"Fine. What's up?"

"Well, as Bree knows, Colin didn't talk to me at all in Science today. He claimed he was paying attention in class, but I didn't try to talk to him while we were working, so I know he was lying. I went to English class and Roger Lopez started saying this mean stuff to me about Colin and asking if I was a bad girl. He's really a jerk! So I asked if I could go to the nurse's office because I was feeling sick to my stomach."

"I'm sorry, Em," Beth said, "but I think maybe you should forget about Colin. Is he really worth all this trouble?"

"Carson Wilde was talking about you in History," Bree announced.

I whipped my head around to look at her. "When were you going to tell me about this?"

"It just happened today, so I was going to tell you on the bus, but you weren't there."

"What did he say?"

"He was talking to Ryan Freeley. He said that you look really cute this year, and that he was thinking about asking you out."

"Oh my gosh! I can't believe this!"

"What did Ryan say?" Beth asked.

"Well..." Bree looked like she didn't want to tell us.

"What?" I asked, a little worried.

"He asked Carson why he would waste his time with you when there's so many new girls to choose from. He said that you are old news and Carson should move on."

"How rude! I never liked Ryan. He thinks he's so cool because his mom was in a music video about a hundred years ago," Beth exaggerated.

"He's a jerk to everyone," Bree said.

"You don't know the half of it. He is spreading around this rumor that Carson and I made out last year at the zoo," I said.

"I heard that, too. Jake Tamlin and some other guy were talking about it in my history class," Beth said. "I told them it was a lie, but I don't think they believed me."

I sighed. "Do you think it was Carson that started it all?"

"No. I think Ryan made it up. You should sue him like celebrities sue the gossip magazines. Bree, your parents are lawyers. Do you think she has a case?"

Bree was looking pretty sad.

"What's wrong, Bree? You've been acting kind of weird lately."

"It's nothing. Just my parents. They've been fighting a lot and it's really getting on my nerves. I don't even want to be at home most of the time."

"Are they going to get a divorce?" I asked. I thought it was a logical question.

"No! Just because they fight sometimes, doesn't mean they don't love each other anymore!"

"Emily, how could you say something like that?" Beth asked.

"I'm sorry! I didn't mean to make anyone mad." I didn't want to fight with Bree again, but this was the way our friendship had always been. Fight, make up, fight, make up.

"Well, think before you speak," Beth said.

"It's alright. I don't know what's going to happen, but I don't think it's that serious," Bree didn't look mad and I was relieved.

"It's probably nothing, Bree. Maybe they're just stressed out at work. If I had to spend that much time with one person, I would probably fight with them, too," Beth said. She was so much like her mom sometimes and other times, they were complete opposites.

"You're right. It's probably about work," Bree said, nodding.

Bree's parents have their own law firm, Marquette Law. I guess in the beginning, they thought it would be nice to work together, but Beth was right. Too much of one person has to drive you crazy.

"Did you ask them about it?" I asked Bree.

"Yeah. I asked my mom why they were fighting one time and she just said it was grown up stuff and I wouldn't understand."

Beth and I rolled our eyes. "Remind me never to be a grown up," Beth said.

"Some grown ups are cool. My aunt, Jody, is cool. Your mom and dad are cool. Even your grandma is cool," I said to Beth.

"Your Aunt Jody IS cool. How come we don't see her anymore?" Bree asked.

"Didn't I tell you? She went to help find homes for the dogs that were in that big hurricane last month."

"That's so awesome!" Beth said. "She is way cooler than my mom."

"She's younger, too, though, and she doesn't have any kids. It's easier to be cool when you don't have to be a mom all the time."

"So, what are you gonna do about Carson and Colin?" Beth asked.

I sighed. I had no idea.

God, what should I do?

Chapter 15
Deal Breaker

True to our word, Eve and I were very sweet to my dad- for awhile anyway. The weekend before the parties, Eve blew it.

I had been thinking about what we were going to say to my dad to get out of our punishment in time for the parties and I went into Eve's room. I had forgotten to knock again and I found her getting dressed. Her hair was fixed and she had on a lot of makeup. To top it off, she was putting on her favorite outfit.

"Eve, what are you doing?" I asked. It was after 10 o'clock. Even if she wasn't grounded, my dad wouldn't have let her go out this late.

"I can't take this anymore, Em. I'm climbing the walls! Price's cousin, Trent, just got his driver's license. He's taking us to Willett," Eve whispered.

My heart nearly jumped out of my chest. Willett was a city about an hour away from Harvey. It was pretty much just one big party. We'd heard so many stories about fights and drugs. It was no place for teenagers to hang out.

"What?" I whispered.

"Price's cousin is taking us to Willett."

"I heard you. What I meant to say was "WHAT?!"

"Look, Emily. You can't tell anyone about this."

"This is dangerous."

"C'mon, Em. Be my sister. Go distract mom and dad while I sneak out," Eve begged. I didn't want to, but I agreed.

"Mom! Dad!" I yelled, running through the house looking for them.

"What is it, Emmy?" my mom asked, her nose in a book, as usual.

I can't find my angel costume. We're supposed to dress up for school the day before Halloween. Will you help me find it?"

They followed me to the basement and I pretended to look through boxes.

"Well, it's right here in the box labeled, 'Halloween'," my mom said, holding up my costume from the year before. "Didn't you think to look there?"

I couldn't sleep that night, thinking and worrying about Eve. The stories that we'd heard about Willett were true. My parents hated the other side of Harvey and they were snobs about it, but Willett was a different story. Willett was dangerous, especially for out of town visitors.

Please, God, please don't let anything bad happen to Eve.

I listened for Eve to come home, but I heard nothing. I even got up a few times to see if she was home, but no one answered when I knocked on her door. I finally fell asleep around 2:30, but the phone woke me up. My heart started to beat fast and loud as I strained my ears to hear my father's side of the conversation.

"You're where? What?! Oh my- Heather! Come in here!" my dad called for my mom. I ran to my door and opened it just enough to see out into the hall where my dad was standing in his robe, one hand holding the phone to his ear, the other on his hip. My mom shuffled down the hall sleepily.

"What is it, dear?" She yawned.

"It's Eve. She and Price are in Willett."

"Oh, dear God! Willett?" My mom went into hysterics.

"Calm down, Heather! I can't hear Eve. Eve, what did you just say?" There was a pause, then, "Stolen car? Are you kidding me with this? You are in deep, Eve, very deep trouble."

"Oh, dear God!" my mom repeated.

"Sit tight, both of you. I'll get there as soon as I can," my dad said and hung up the phone.

"What's going on, Kevin?" my mom demanded.

"Our daughter snuck out of the house to go to Willett with Price and his cousin who, apparently had stolen a car to get there. The police caught the boy and he's sitting in jail while Eve and Price have no way to get home. They're at the police station right now. I'm going to go get them. I don't want that moron, Frank McCloskey, to go. I don't trust him with our daughter any more than I trust his son!"

"Just let me throw some sweats on. I'll just be a minute," my mom said, heading for her bedroom.

"No, no. You stay here. Someone needs to stay here in case Dana wakes up."

"I'll wake Emily. She can do it. I'll go crazy waiting for you here."

"No, let Emily sleep. Eve will be fine. Don't worry so much," my dad said and kissed my mom on the cheek. After he left, my mom sat down and cried.

I went to her and hugged her. "Mom, she'll be alright. Won't she?"

My mom didn't answer. She just held me and rocked back and forth.

God, it's all my fault. I never should have helped her sneak out. Please let her be ok.

I'd never really thought about it before, but Eve was making my parents miserable. She was always getting into trouble, always making them angry or worried. As I looked at my mom, I decided I never wanted to be the reason she looked like that. I never wanted to give her a reason to cry so hard.

So much for our plan of being sweet and innocent to get out of our punishment. Eve wasn't going to get to go to the party at Priddy Park. Eve wasn't going anywhere anytime soon.

At around 5 o'clock Sunday morning, Eve's bedroom door slammed shut and I heard her crying, but I didn't go to check on her. For the first time, I really understood my parents and I believed Eve deserved her punishment.

Chapter 16
Carson

Sunday morning, we all got up to go to church, just the same as every other Sunday. We all did except for Eve, that is. She was protesting.

"Eve! You get out of bed, get dressed, and join us at church," my dad yelled through the door. My mom, Dana, and I were waiting in the living room.

"No!" Eve answered my dad.

"It's not a request, Eve!"

I moved to the hallway so I could watch. My mom didn't notice. She was trying to calm Dana down, who was making a fuss about her dress being too tight. I could tell by the way she was grabbing at it.

Eve's door flew open. She was wearing the same outfit she had worn to Willett the night before. Her mascara was running all down her face from crying. "I am not going to church with you today or any other day. I'm quitting school and I'm moving in with Sara. I'm tired of your stupid rules and your stupid punishments." She gave my dad a little shove and he made a move toward her. I sucked in my breath, because I thought he might hit her, but instead he turned around and walked a couple steps away from her, running his fingers through his hair.

"You are fifteen years old. You can't make those decisions. You will live in my house until you are at least 18," my dad said, trying to be calm.

"No, I will not! Why should I stay? You don't care about me. You have your angel and your princess. Then there's me, the black sheep of the family."

"You know that isn't true. Don't try to make yourself the victim here. What you did was wrong!"

"If you weren't so over-the-top about things, I would have asked for permission to go to Willett. Price's mom knew where we were going. I didn't know the car was stolen, and neither did Price. We told you that on the way home. This is crazy! I feel like I can't have a normal teenage life. I can't do anything my friends do."

"Sneaking out didn't help. Are you any closer now to being able to do what your friends do? No, because you're grounded and you deserved your punishment."

"I do? I deserve to have the boy I love taken away from me?" She looked at me then, "That's right, Emily. This is what you have to look forward to. Dad has forbidden me to see Price outside of school ever again." She turned back to my dad. "Well, I don't have to take this. When you get back from church, I won't be here."

I guess my dad thought she was just being dramatic, because he stormed out the door and we followed.

It was hard to concentrate on the sermon with all that had happened at home. I watched Dana as she colored in her coloring book.

After church someone tapped me on the shoulder. I turned around. It was Carson.

"Hey Carson! I didn't see you in church," I said, surprised.

"Yeah, we came in late. My little brother gave my mom a hard time this morning. He's such a brat!" Carson explained.

"How do you like school?"

"I'd like it a lot more if we had some classes together." Carson smiled and blushed.

"I need to ask you something, Carson."

"What's up?"

"I heard that there's a rumor going around that we made out at the zoo last year."

"I heard that, too. I wasn't the one who started that rumor." Carson looked sincere and I believed him. I never thought he was the type of guy to spread rumors.

"I know it was Ryan Freeley, but did you tell Ryan that we made out?"

"Ryan saw me kiss you. He made the rest of the story up. I tried to tell him that nothing else happened, but he didn't believe me. I think he really believes his own made up version."

"I never liked Ryan anyway. I am so glad it wasn't you that started that dumb rumor."

"Emily, do you have a boyfriend?" Colin asked, after clearing his throat three times.

"Well, I sort of had a potential boyfriend, but I don't anymore."

"I don't have a girlfriend, either." Carson was smiling the same smile he had the year before when he kissed my cheek at the zoo.

"I have to go, Carson. My parents are coming and I'm grounded. I don't wanna get in any more trouble."

Carson said hello to my parents and winked at me as we walked away. I smiled broadly.

Who needs Colin?

When we got home from church, Eve was gone. My mom cried, my dad was angry, and Dana and I could do nothing but go to our rooms and give them a chance to talk. I turned on my television and pretended to watch, but all I could think about was Eve.

Dear God, I feel so guilty and helpless. Where is Eve? Please bring her home. Breathe. Positive white light.

Chapter 17
The Deal

My dad came into my room before I got up on Monday morning. He sat down on the side of my bed and sighed. "I guess you're pretty worried about Eve, huh?"

I nodded.

"Do you understand why I grounded you?"

"Because we lied to you?"

"Well, yes, because you lied, but there's another reason. You know how I feel about dating. You know the rule. You can't date until high school."

"It wasn't really a date, Daddy. We were with a bunch of people from school in a well lit public place."

"That's all fine, but you still know the rule."

"Do you have to be so strict?"

"Can we make a deal?" I nodded. "How about I agree not to be so strict about hanging out at Harvey Mall if you agree to have a chaperone when you're with a boy."

"Ok, it's a deal," I said, shaking his hand, "but only until high school."

He laughed. "Alright. When you're in high school, you can drop the chaperone."

"Dad, what's going to happen with Eve?"

"Eve is at Sara's, just like she said she'd be, but Sara's mom told her she could just stay a couple days, and then she's going to come home. The situation is under control. Don't worry anymore," my dad said, touching my cheek.

"Do you think you could make a deal with Eve, too?"

"We both said some things we didn't mean. She just needs some time to cool down, and so do I."

He started to walk out of the room and I remembered the party, "Dad, can I ask for a favor?"

"What is it, Emmy Lou?"

"There is a chaperoned party on Saturday at Priddy Park. I really want to go."

My dad thought for a minute and said, "You can go."

I smiled, but I felt sorry for Eve. If she had just stuck with the plan, she might have gotten to go to her party too.

Chapter 18
Lizzie

As if Colin hadn't been enough of a jerk, I walked into class on Monday and found out I was sitting with someone new. It was so obvious that Colin asked to move because he doesn't like me. That didn't stop him from watching to see how I would react, though. I just looked at him and shook my head.

"Hi Emily!" The girl I was sitting next to had blond hair like me, but she had blue streaks running through it. My parents would kill me if I came home with hair like that. It was cool, though, in a weird way. I recognized the girl from lunch, where she always sat with Cheyenne, who always had something different going on with her hair, makeup, or clothes.

"Hi," I answered, embarrassed that I didn't know her name.

"My name is Lizzie. We never met, because I used to sit in the back of the room."

"You mean, where Colin is sitting now?" I tried to sound like I didn't care.

"Yeah. What's up with that? Why did he ask to have his seat changed?" Lizzie asked, her head cocked to the side. She chewed her gum like a cow.

I shrugged. "He doesn't know how to act like a human being."

"Mr. Greesy's been wanting a reason to split me and Cheyenne up anyway." Lizzie said, popping her gum.

"So, now Cheyenne is sitting next to Colin. Poor girl!"

Lizzie gave me a funny look, but I didn't have time to explain myself. The bell rang and Mr. Greesy was ready to start class. Lizzie put her gum in some tissue and wadded it up. It looked like she had been chewing a whole pack at once.

Mr. Greesy asked a lot of questions about the lesson and I found out that Lizzie was really smart. She raised her hand to answer every question.

Lizzie and I finished our assignments early, so we had extra time before class was over. I pulled out a notebook and wrote down the whole story about Colin and handed it to Lizzie. She read it and wrote back, "What a jerk! A friend of Colin's asked me to go to the party with him. I hope he's not a jerk too."

A part of me hoped it was Roger she was talking about, because I would have loved to tell her about all the silly, childish things he'd done out of jealousy. I wrote, "Which friend?"

My heart sank as I read her answer. Kenny Torn. Lauren's crush.

The bell rang and I quickly got up. I crumbled up the letter and threw it away.

"Emily, wait!" I heard Lizzie behind me.

"Yeah, really, why are you walking so fast?" Bree asked, when I didn't wait for her and Jasmine.

"You got a date?" Jasmine asked.

"No."

"Well, I do. I have to meet Dwayne. I'll see y'all later," Jasmine announced.

"She is so lucky!" Lizzie said, watching Jasmine walk away. Turning to me, she asked, "What's up?"

"Lizzie, I don't think we can be friends."

"Why not?"

"I guess you don't know. I'm friends with Lauren McCloskey."

Lizzie shrugged and shook her head, "What does that mean? I barely know her."

"It means we can't be friends." Bree and I left Lizzie standing in the hallway. She was probably wondering what was going on. I didn't know if she knew that Lauren liked Kenny or not, but that wasn't the point. I knew. I felt bad about hurting Lizzie's feelings, but I would feel worse if Lauren saw her and Kenny together at the party and then found out I had become friends with her.

"Wow, that was kinda harsh, Emily," Bree said, when we were out of earshot.

"She's going to the party with Kenny Torn. I didn't know what else to do. I didn't want to just come right out and say that Lauren has a crush on Kenny. Lauren would kill me!"

"That's true," Bree agreed.

"Now I have to worry about Lauren getting hurt. She's going to freak when she sees them together."

Hi God. What do I do now?

Chapter 19

Heartbreak

Lauren was her usual cheerful self when I walked into English class.

"Em! Come here, quick! I have to tell you something." She looked so excited.

"What's up?" I asked. I was finding it hard to decide whether or not to tell her about Kenny and Lizzie.

"In art class last hour, I was hinting to Kenny that I wanted him to ask me to the party. I really think he's going to. I just think he's nervous."

"Oh, Lauren, you didn't!"

"Why?"

"I have to tell you something, but I don't want you to get hurt."

"Well, it's too late now. You're going to have to tell me whether or not it hurts. If you were that concerned about my feelings, you wouldn't have brought it up at all."

"No, it's not like that. I think you have a right to know and you're going to find out somehow, so it might as well be from me."

"So, what is it?"

I stumbled on my words, but they finally came out right, "Lauren, I just found out that Kenny asked Lizzie Blaine to the party." I closed my eyes as Lauren turned pale- paler than usual.

"Lizzie Blaine?" Lauren mumbled, then yelled, "She's a freak!"

Mrs. Whitney frowned at Lauren, but she didn't do anything because the bell hadn't rung yet.

"Lauren, you have to calm down or you're going to get into trouble with Mrs. Whitney."

"No, I won't. I'm fine." The rest of the day, she was quiet. She was too quiet. That's how I knew she was upset.

On the bus home, I told Dwayne about the situation and he had an idea. "My step-brother, Ty, is in the 10th grade. I'll bet he would take Lauren to make Kenny jealous," Dwayne suggested.

"I'll call Lauren when I get home, and ask her what she thinks of it."

"Wait until I talk to Ty. Give me your number and I'll call you after I talk to him."

Later that night, Dwayne called. He had the whole thing set up. We just needed Lauren to be ok with it. I called her and she was more than ok with it. She was so excited to be going to a party with a guy in high school, even if it was fake.

I was happy for her, but also sad that I didn't have a date. It helped to think that maybe Carson would be there. I didn't need to show up with a date in order to have fun. I hoped Colin was going, because I planned on having a good time and being the life of the party. I was going to show Colin that I didn't care that he had stopped liking me.

Chapter 20

The Party

I was so excited the day of the party. I wasn't even upset anymore that Colin had asked to have his seat changed in Science.

Bree, Beth, Jasmine, Dwayne, and I met at the entrance to Priddy Park and we walked together to the small lake where everyone was supposed to go. We were all dressed up in our costumes. Bree was a ghost, Beth was a witch, Jasmine was a pirate, Dwayne was the devil, and I was an angel.

Music played from a giant boom box that was guarded by a police officer named Brady, who was a friend of my dad's from high school. They still went out to the bar together every Friday night.

"Hi Brady!" I waved. I knew my dad would ask him if I had behaved.

"Hey, Emmy," he answered.

Carson came up behind me and pulled my hair gently. "Hi angel," he said.

"Hi Carson. What are you supposed to be?"

He laughed. "I guess I'm a guy. I couldn't figure out a good costume." He was dressed in his normal clothes.

"If anyone asks, just tell them you're dressed as an eighth grader."

"Emily, you are so cute."

I blushed. He was always so bold.

While we were dancing, I noticed Colin. He was dressed up as a vampire. He was looking at me, but looked away when I looked at him. I decided I wasn't going to play this game anymore.

"Carson, I have to do something," I said.

I walked right up to Colin and asked, "Why are you being such a jerk?"

"I'm not trying to be a jerk."

"Well, you are."

"So what? What do you want from me?"

"I want to know why you stopped talking to me. We had a great time at the mall and then you started ignoring me and even had your seat moved."

He looked away. "It's because of Roger."

"Because of Roger?!"

"Roger is my friend. Roger likes you."

"I don't like Roger. Ok? Do you get that? Whether or not you go out with me, I am not going out with Roger. I think he's an idiot and I can't stand to be around him."

"Well, I guess, when you put it that way, there's no reason why we can't go out. I mean, he'll be mad at me, but I guess he'll get over it."

"He'll have to get over it, Colin. Not everything is about Roger. He can find someone else."

Colin and I danced together. He was a good dancer, even in the long, black cloak. My favorites were the slow songs when I put my arms around his neck and his hands were on my sides and we swayed back and forth.

"Colin, I have to do something." I knew I had to say something to Carson. He was probably wondering what happened. I looked all over and finally found him dancing with Christa. I turned to go back to Colin. I had no right to be mad at Carson. I chose Colin.

I looked around, again, trying to find Kenny and Lizzie, but I didn't see them. I wondered if Lizzie had changed her mind.

"What's wrong, Emily?" Colin asked.

"Nothing's wrong. Why?"

"You act like you're looking for someone. Were you supposed to meet someone else?"

"No, I was looking for Kenny."

"Why?"

"Do you promise you won't tell him?"

"I promise."

"Lauren likes Kenny and I found out that he's coming to the party with Lizzie Blaine." I immediately felt guilty for telling him.

"They might not show up, Emily."

"Why not?"

"How well do you know Lizzie?"

"Not very well. We sit next to each other now in Science, but we don't talk much at all since I told her we couldn't be friends."

"Lizzie Blaine will do anything to get people to like her, especially guys. Everyone knows she's not a virgin anymore. That's why Kenny asked her out."

I shook my head. "No, Colin, that is so wrong! I may not know her very well, but she's a nice girl."

Colin shrugged. "I'm just telling you what I heard. She has kissed a lot of guys and Roger said that she took her shirt off for him."

I rolled my eyes. "You believe Roger?"

Colin shrugged again, but he didn't say anything.

Out the corner of my eye, I saw Lauren. She was dressed up as Cinderella and Ty was Prince Charming. I was so happy for her, I was about to burst!

"What? What's going on?" Colin asked.

"C'mon. I have to talk to Lauren." I pulled Colin by the arm to where Lauren was. As I got closer, I saw that she had found Kenny and Lizzie. Kenny was looking a little jealous. Maybe he didn't like Lauren, but he didn't want her to like someone else.

"Kenny, this is Ty," Lauren was saying.

"Do you go to Harvey Middle?" Kenny asked.

"No, I go to Harvey High," Ty said, with a low voice.

"Hi Lauren! Hey Ty! What's up guys?" I asked, barging into the conversation.

"Hi Em! I was just introducing Ty to Kenny and...Lizzie?" Lauren pretended not to know her.

"Yeah, it's Lizzie," Lizzie said, softly. She had no idea what was going on.

"Oh! Ty, I think I left my tiara in your car!" Lauren exclaimed. I had trouble holding back the laughter. A tiara? A car? She was really laying it on thick.

When Lauren and Ty left, I looked at Lizzie. She was a nice girl. She hadn't done anything wrong. I felt bad for her if what Colin had said was true. Kenny was going to try to take advantage of her. He was one of the guys Mrs. Glass warned me about.

About half an hour later, I saw Kenny and Lizzie walking toward the baseball diamond.

"Lizzie!" I yelled.

She turned to look at me, but didn't stop walking.

"Emily, what are you going to do?" Colin asked.

"I'm going to get Lizzie away from Kenny, that's what I'm going to do. He doesn't deserve Lauren and he doesn't deserve Lizzie."

I ran after Lizzie, and Colin ran after me.

"Lizzie, I need to talk to you," I said, gasping for air.

"No, you don't. Colin, do me a favor and get your girlfriend out of here," Kenny said. I really couldn't stand him.

Lizzie pulled away from Kenny and I grabbed her arm and led her to a park bench.

"Lizzie, Kenny thinks-" I started. I wasn't sure what to say, maybe it was none of my business.

"Kenny thinks what?"

"Kenny brought you here because he thinks you'll do stuff with him."

"Stuff?"

"Kissing and other stuff."

Lizzie laughed. "Well, I already kissed him. What's the big deal about that?"

"I think it's more of the other stuff that he wants."

"No, he doesn't! He was just going to show me the dugout, that's all."

"Lizzie! He was taking you there so no one could see you guys!"

"Just mind your own business, Emily!" Lizzie went back to Kenny and they went in the dugout.

I shook my head. "Remind me to tell Lauren what Kenny's really like."

When the sun started to go down, Colin and I snuck away from the crowd and watched the sunset over the lake. It was so pretty.

"Can I kiss you, Emily?" Colin asked.

"Yes," I answered, shyly.

He bent down and his lips touched mine. I felt a tingle run through my body and butterflies in my tummy. When he pulled away, he touched his forehead to mine and said, "Wow." I giggled and pulled him into a hug. My first kiss. I was so glad it was with Colin.

When I looked passed Colin, I saw Brady watching. I began to worry, but he just grinned and nodded at me. He was pretty cool.

Later that evening, I went home still floating on air, my head still in the clouds. Eve was waiting for me outside my bedroom. She had come home the day before and found that not much had changed. She was still grounded. The only thing that had changed was that my parents were going to let her keep dating Price. "Emily, you have to help me convince dad to let me go to the game and the party tomorrow."

I just shook my head and went in my room and put a chair in front of the door. I flopped down on the bed and giggled, looking at the ceiling.

"Not now, Eve. Tonight is all about the luckiest girl in Harvey," I said. "It's all about me."

i want morebooks!

Buy your books fast and straightforward online - at one of world's fastest growing online book stores! Environmentally sound due to Print-on-Demand technologies.

Buy your books online at
www.get-morebooks.com

Kaufen Sie Ihre Bücher schnell und unkompliziert online – auf einer der am schnellsten wachsenden Buchhandelsplattformen weltweit! Dank Print-On-Demand umwelt- und ressourcenschonend produziert.

Bücher schneller online kaufen
www.morebooks.de

VDM Verlagsservicegesellschaft mbH
Heinrich-Böcking-Str. 6-8
D - 66121 Saarbrücken

Telefon: +49 681 3720 174
Telefax: +49 681 3720 1749

info@vdm-vsg.de
www.vdm-vsg.de

Made in the USA
Lexington, KY
17 June 2012